Christmas Fever

P.L. Harris

COPYRIGHT

This book is a work of fiction. The names, characters, places and incidents are products of the writer's imagination or have been used fictitiously and are not to be constructed as real. Any resemblance to persons, living or dead, actual events, locale or organisations is entirely coincidental.

Published by Gumnut Press

Copyright © 2018 P.L. Harris

ISBN: 978-0-6483729-3-6

Edited by Nina S. Gooden
(www.greenteaandpinkink.com)

Cover by Beetiful (www.beetifulbookcovers.com)

All Rights Are Reserved. No part of this book may be used or reproduced in any form by any electronic, mechanical, or any other device now known or invented hereafter without permission of the author, except in the case of brief quotations embodied in critical articles and reviews.

These forms include, but are not limited to xerography, photocopy, scanning, recording, distributing via internet means, informational storage and retrieval system.

Because of the dynamic nature of the internet, any web address or links contained in this book may have changed since publication and may no longer be valid.

DEDICATION

For Cassandra

Follow your dreams.

ALSO BY P.L. HARRIS

Lovers of Love
Callie's Dilemma
Second Chance at Love
Christmas Fever
Mask of Desire
Juliet's Kiss

Lovers of Mystery and Suspense
Hidden Secrets – Young Adult

Amateur Sleuths
<u>The Cupcake Capers Cozy Mystery Series</u>
Cupcakes and Cyanide
Cupcakes and Curses
Cupcakes and Corpses

Publishers Stocking P.L. Harris Books

Amazon

Serenity Press

Gumnut Press

Barnes and Noble

Blue Swan Publishing

Evernight Publishing

Making Magic Happen Academy

Chapter One

DEEP BREATHS, TESSA. Deep breaths.

Tessa Quinn's gut tightened as she pulled into the driveway of her mother's Tudor-style home.

It was an icy four degrees outside the car, but her sweaty palms soaked the inside of her new woollen gloves. She gripped the steering wheel and waited for the storm in her stomach to settle. The same storm erupted the moment she'd returned home to Whittaker Springs last week.

It had been six years since she'd left. Six long years of trying to make it as an actor in London. Six long years of failed romances and missed Christmases. Whittaker Springs still looks as wonderful now as it had the day she walked out on her life. Regret flooded her heart.

Tessa headed up the garden path, fumbling in her handbag for her house keys. The overgrown Holly bush stabbed her leg as she walked past. "Ouch," she groaned, then chuckled to herself. *Just like the old days.*

She paused at the top of the stairs and glanced across the barren yard. Bland and empty. Void of the usual Christmas decorations her mother insisted on displaying each year. She supressed the sudden pang of guilt churning deep in the pit of her stomach. Their house usually came alive at Christmas. It was always the best decorated house in the street. She could hear her mother's words in her head, "If you're going to do it, do it once and do it to perfection."

I hate to continue to be a disappointment, Mum, but perfection was not something I was born with.

She entered the house, the sharp click of the door closing behind her disturbing her thoughts. The cold, sterile air hit Tessa square in the chest as she moved through the hallway toward the kitchen. Her bag landed with a thud on the kitchen table. The same table her mother slaved over, year after year, to make the perfect Christmas pudding. The same table she'd drawn flowers on when she was five. Tessa smiled, remembering the beetroot-red colour of her mother's face when she walked in and caught her in the act.

What was she going to do with the house, now that her mother was too sick to live here alone? *I could move back home and take care of you, but what do I know about the debilitating effects of dementia? I'm no nurse.*

Her hands crept up her arms as her gaze swept the kitchen and living room. It seemed so…stagnant and desolate. Her mother's perfection used to reign from every angle. *Everything in its place and a place for everything.* Except, now, chaos engulfed every corner. The evidence of her mother's ill health hit hard, like a sledge hammer. *Oh, Mum, how could I have been so ignorant to not see this coming?*

Tessa jumped at the high-pitched ring of her mobile. *Great, now what?* "Hello, Tessa speaking."

"Tessa, it's Sophie. Ahhhhhhhhh," she squealed in Tessa's ear. "I can't believe you're finally here, and just in time for the Christmas celebrations. Why didn't you call me as soon as you were back in town?"

Because I was embarrassed and didn't want to face up to being a failure, especially to my best friend. That's why.

'I'm sorry, Sophie. I haven't been back long and I've been busy sorting out the stuff with Mum and—"

"I want to know everything. John's flat-out working for his new promotion and I've got my two little cherubs booked in for day care tomorrow, so let's do lunch and you can tell me all about it. I can't wait to see you."

Tessa felt sick to the bottom of her stomach. She used to tell Sophie everything before she'd left town. It was easier to bend the truth on a phone call from London, but now seeing her face to face, Sophie would work out she was lying in an instant. *I guess there's no use putting off the inevitable.*

"Sure," Tessa said. "Lunch tomorrow sounds great. Where shall I meet you?"

"How about Tony's Bar and Grill?" She asked. "I'm sure you remember it. Tony's made a special effort with the new Christmas menu this year, you'll love it."

Tessa's heart tore in two at the mention of Tony's Bar and Grill. It had been the place to hang out in high school, and the place she'd first laid eyes on Blake. She pushed the unwanted feeling of loss aside and rolled back her shoulders, determined to show Sophie the past was buried deep in her heart. Her future was now focused on her mother.

"Tony's sounds great. Shall we say midday?"

"Midday sounds perfect," Sophie said. "I'll meet you in our usual booth. It'll be just like old times."

Yeah, just like old times. Guilt shot up Tessa's spine. "Midday it is, then," she said ending the call. It had been Sophie who'd encouraged her to pursue her acting career, otherwise she may never have left Whittaker Springs at all.

Looking in the direction of the oven, she sighed. "Well, dinner isn't going to cook itself." As she prepared her dinner, her mind buzzed with the list of things to do before heading back to the hospital for her evening visit.

One: pack Mum a change of clothes. Two: when I get back to the hospital, see Mum's doctor to get an update. Three: call the gardener. Four: check Mum's finances.

Firstly, she busied herself making one of her favourite dishes, lasagne. She put the finishing touches on and popped it in the oven. Tessa sifted through the mail she'd thrown on the kitchen bench earlier that day.

"Bills, bills, junk mail. More bills," she said, sighing. "I don't know how long it's going to take me to get your finances in order, Mum, but I guess they're my problem now."

The blood froze in her veins. Her name splayed across the envelope in bold letters. Tessa's eyes stared at the words plastered in red print on the top of the envelope; *Whittaker Springs High School Christmas Reunion.*

You can't be serious? Like I don't have enough complications in my life right now.

Whittaker Springs thrived on the Christmas spirit. December had always been a special time of year for Tessa. Somehow, six years of Christmases in London seemed to have stolen the joy in her heart. No love and no Blake.

Scanning the invite, her chest tightened as if someone had squeezed the air from her lungs with their bare hands. *This Saturday evening.* Why couldn't it have been two weeks ago, before she'd arrived back in town? Everyone would be there, eager to know all about her life as an actor on the West End, sucking every tidbit of information out of her. The awful part was knowing she'd have to see Blake and he'd probably have a wife by his side. Her worst nightmare come true.

How could she face everyone? "They all thought I'd make it in London." She huffed, "What would they say if I told them I bombed out on the stage years ago and now I teach drama?" Tessa's heart burst with pride, remembering her students up on stage performing in her latest pantomime. *Guess the old saying still lives. Those that can't do, teach.*

She scrunched the invitation up and tossed it in the waste basket. "Well, that takes care of that. If I don't go, I don't have to deal with it. Problem solved." She smiled to herself.

After dinner, Tessa made quick work of the dishes and headed back to the hospital. A twinge of envy scuttled up her spine as she drove down streets, seeing every house decorated with Christmas lights. Tessa envied the hassle-free life Whittaker Springs offered. She loved growing up here, but she'd always imagined herself living the high life abroad, with Blake.

The sterile odour of the hospital assaulted Tessa from every angle. She held her breath, hoping it would pass. Her mouth tasted like metal for hours after a visit. Watching her mother being slowly eaten away by debilitating dementia gutted Tessa. It was not exactly the homecoming she was prepared for. Maybe, just maybe, it wasn't too late to right some of her wrongs.

Tessa's heart broke for all the wasted time, spent over the years, bickering back and forth with her mother about senseless, petty issues that could have been resolved in minutes. If only she had been able to discuss them with her, instead of turning most conversations into screaming matches. Maybe she wouldn't feel so guilty, praying for more time to make things right between them.

Walking into her mother's ward, she ignored the niggling feeling of regret that had planted itself deep in her gut. "Time to move forward with my life, and that means sorting things out for Mum. Hopefully, that doesn't involve staying in Whittaker Springs a moment longer than I have to."

"So, Lyndall, do you think Tessa will like these blue orchids? I think they'll bring out her eyes, don't you?"

Outside her mother's room, the echo of her name froze Tessa to the spot. *That sounds like Isaac?* Her brow creased. *Why would he be bringing me flowers?*

She'd met Isaac on her first visit to the hospital and they'd quickly become friends. She'd walked into her mother's room to see a tall, robust man, decked out in a nurse's uniform, staring at her with inquisitive eyes. He was a little on the slim side but what he lacked in muscle, he more than made up for in the looks department. Apparently, he was a new face around the hospital.

"Tessa?" The crackle in Lyndall's soft voice made her words barely audible.

"Yes, Lyndall. Tessa, your daughter. She was in earlier today visiting."

"She was?"

"Yes. She's a beautiful young lady, you should be very proud of her."

Tessa's stomach revolted at his comment. *Proud. Are you proud of me, Mum?*

'I brought these flowers for her. I thought they might cheer her up. She has the most gorgeous sapphire blue eyes I've ever seen."

Oh, my God. Nervous tension shot through her spine. A relationship with her mother's nurse was completely out of the question. *It was wrong. He's my mother's nurse, for God's sake.*

She hadn't meant to lead Isaac on, but it seems she had without even knowing it. A smile edged the corner of her mouth. Butterflies started doing backflips on top of backflips in her stomach and she wanted to jump up in the air and do a fist pump. Men hadn't found her attractive in a while and it felt good, damn good. Maybe she was reading it all wrong.

"I'm sure she will love them," Lyndall said softly. "I'm tired."

"Why don't you snuggle down for the night and I'll shoot off as soon as I have these flowers the way I want them?"

Lyndall sighed. "See you tomorrow?"

"Of course, you're my number one patient."

Tessa peered around the door frame, just enough to see Isaac tuck the blankets up under her mother's chin. "Now try and get some sleep."

She watched Isaac pause beside the bed and it wasn't long before Lyndall's heavy breathing filled the small room.

Tessa cleared her throat and headed in. "Isaac, how nice to see you again." She smiled, placing her mother's bag on the chair beside her bed.

His eyes followed her entrance like a hawk. "Tessa. Back so soon?"

"I didn't realise you'd still be working."

He held his finger to his lips in a shushing action and pointed to Lyndall, who was already deep in slumber. "Actually," he said in a quiet voice. "I finished an hour ago but I wanted to drop these orchids off for you. They reminded me of your eyes, and they add a little more joy to the room," he said, fiddling with the vase placement on the counter. "I thought they might cheer you up."

Tessa smiled. She liked Isaac. He did have great taste in flowers, not to mention his backside looked incredibly hot in tight jeans. Her chest tightened as she sucked in a deep breath. "The orchids are lovely, thank you. As you know, I haven't been back in town long." She shuffled from one foot to another. What was wrong with her? She'd never had a problem talking to a man before.

His eyebrow raised. "I know. This will be my first Christmas in Whittaker Springs and I hear it's the best time of year. I love how the whole town gets involved. The excitement is contagious. I especially love the cute snowman near the rotunda. Do you know he gets a new outfit every day?"

Tessa's nervous hands twisted in front of her. "Yes, yes, I do. That has been a Whittaker Springs tradition as far back as I can remember," she said. "Listen, Isaac, I appreciate you listening to me babble since I've been visiting Mum."

"No problem," he chuckled. "I have been told that I'm a good listener once or twice before."

Cute, and a good listener. Maybe I've won the lottery, but he is no Blake.

"It's just that I haven't really talked openly to anyone since coming back to town. I'm not intending to stay long so I'm kind of keeping to myself, so I'd appreciate it if you—"

His brow creased. "What do you mean, you're not staying long? I thought you moved back to take care of your mum?"

"Yes, I moved back to sort out my mum's affairs and work out what's the best option for her health, moving forward. I have a job back in London, one I love, and at the moment I'm on leave—"

"But no one there who loves you?" Isaac butted in.

Isaac's words were like rubbing salt in an open wound. *Worst mistake of my life.* Her decision to leave everyone behind, including Blake, still haunted her thoughts.

"For a newcomer like me, finding a friend in a small town like Whittaker Springs is hard. Everyone wants to know your business and I'm not exactly ready to share the ins and outs of my life with everyone just yet."

"What do you mean?" she asked.

"It's not important," he said under his breath. "I just meant that when you move from the city to a small town, people tend to make judgements about you before they really get to know you. Judgements about your life and your past."

Tessa began to unpack the change of clothes she'd brought in for her mother. "I know how fast gossip travels in this town. If I'm a master at anything, it's keeping a secret."

"There's a lot more to that statement than meets the eye. Care to share?"

Cursing, she hurried forward and neatly placed the clothes in the top drawer. "I know you mean well, but my life is...a bit of a mess at the moment."

"Whose life isn't?" Isaac's voice drummed on. "My family didn't really approve of the lifestyle I chose to live."

Tessa frowned.

He shrugged it off, but Tessa caught the pain strewn across his face. "If I wanted to stay a part of *their* family, it was live by their rules or get out. So, here I am."

Her heart sliced in two, remembering how her mother had done the same to her. Her career or Blake. "Yeah, I know exactly how you feel."

"That's why I'm here in Whittaker Springs. A new life, a new start."

Tessa smiled.

"I'm a friendly ear, ready to listen if you need it. I promise it will go to the grave with me." He mimed a zipper closing his lips. "By the sounds of it, you don't have many people to talk to."

You got that right.

Tessa's heart warmed to his trusting eyes. *What harm could it do?*

'Well, you know how sometimes you can bend the truth a little?" She exhaled and sat on the edge of her mother's bed, careful not to disturb her slumber.

Isaac nodded.

"Well, me and my big mouth made all kinds of promises to the townsfolk here, that I'd return a famous actress on the West End. I left town to become an actress and it didn't exactly work out as I planned, and now I'm too ashamed and embarrassed to tell people the truth."

"Believe it or not, I do know how you feel. I know exactly what you mean. From what I hear around town, you're a great actor."

Anger bled through her body. "Stop, just stop, please," she said, rubbing her temples. "That's just it. I bombed out in London. I suck. I'm no great, successful actor. I haven't had an acting job in the past three years. I work in a delicatessen and I teach drama part-time in a small private school, just outside London. Although I love it—the drama teaching, that is, not the delicatessen—it's not exactly what I told everyone when I left."

"Oh."

"Yeah. Oh." Her gut wrenched and weariness crept over her body. "I thought I was the bee's knees, as good as my mother." Tessa gazed warmly at her mother as she slept soundly beside her. "Boy, was I wrong. I got a few good roles, but then it all fell apart. I couldn't even get a job using my mother's name. People didn't know her anymore and I didn't know how to tell her I was a failure. I knew I'd made the wrong choice and I wanted to come home." *To Blake.*

'But she'd bragged to everyone in town about how I was going to be a famous actress. For once, she was proud of me and it felt good. How could I let her down? So, it was easier to just stay away and let her believe in her dream." She hesitated, her chest tightening with an uncomfortable burn. "I thought I'd have plenty of time to come clean and then Mum's condition got worse and then pneumonia set in and" – she shrugged – "here I am."

"So, let me get this straight, you've been working in a delicatessen and teaching drama and no one knew?" Isaac asked.

She nodded. "I love my students. It's a far cry from a West End stage, but after the way I big noted myself before I left, I can't see people understanding when they find out the truth. God, I behaved like a spoilt child."

His eyes widened and then he grinned. "I hope you can get out of it without leaving too much destruction in your wake."

Emotion welled in her chest. "To top it off, I get home today and find an invitation to my high school Christmas reunion in the mail." She chuckled to herself. "How the hell am I supposed to face everyone?"

"Well, it could be a good place to come clean. Since everyone will be there, you can do it in one blow."

Anger tightened Tessa's jaw. "I don't think so. I'll be the laughing stock of the school. Blake will be there and he was right to dump me. That way, he didn't have to watch me make a total fool of myself."

"And Blake is?"

Tessa throat clenched and she struggled to swallow around the lump in her throat. "My high school sweetheart. The man I thought I'd spend the rest of my life with."

"I see," Isaac said sympathetically.

Her lips thinned. Her breathing was heavy. The fight was draining from her body. "I'm sorry, Isaac. I didn't mean to dump all this on you. I guess once I started talking, I couldn't stop."

"No problem. Listening is one of my strengths, or so I'm told, and besides, it's part of a nurse's job to provide comfort for those in need, even the patient's family."

Tessa smiled. "Thanks for listening, but it's my problem to work out." She turned towards her mother's sleeping body. "It looks like she's out for the night. I've kept you here long enough and you're not even on duty."

"No problem," he chuckled. "Listen, if you want to go to this Christmas reunion—"

Tessa cut him off abruptly shaking her head. "No, there's no way I'm going."

"Okay, but if you *want* to, I'd be happy to go with you. It'd be a great way for me to meet a whole bunch of people, or just in case you need a buffer or quick escape."

Something in his voice settled her. "Thank you, Isaac I appreciate the offer."

"All right, I'm out of here." He smiled as he left.

"Well, Mum, it looks like I've really dumped myself in it big time." She re-tucked the blanket around Lyndall's neck. Tessa's cold lips were warmed by her mother's skin as she gave her a tender kiss goodbye. "I wish I could talk to you." Sadness crept into Tessa's heart. "I could really do with your advice. I miss you so much." A tear threatened to drop from her cheek.

"'til tomorrow, Mum."

Chapter Two

BLAKE TOOK A swig of his beer. Six years, he'd been trying to forget the way Tessa trampled his heart. He took one look at her, sitting in their booth across the room, and his heart burned for her, as it always had.

Damn the woman. Who the hell does she think she is, coming back into town like nothing happened between us, like she didn't destroy everything when she left?

"Another beer, Blake?" Tony asked.

Blake nodded. "Sure, why not?"

"So, have you spoken to her yet?" Tony pried, as he placed another schooner of Heady Topper in front of Blake.

Blake's brow furrowed in Tony's direction. "Who?"

"Tessa?" Tony nodded in her direction. "Have you spoken to her yet?"

Blake's eyes followed Tony's. Anger surged through his veins. He was determined to keep his cool and not let on how much he was affected by Tessa's presence. She was still the sexiest woman he'd ever seen, even though he hadn't seen her in six years. He shrugged. "Not yet. I hear she's back to the care of her mum. I'm sure we'll get around to it. It's not as if we can avoid each other in a town this size."

Tessa's bright laugh echoing across the diner tore Blake's heart in two. Why was he here tormenting himself? Just because she was back in town, didn't mean that she could storm back into his life. He took a gulp of his beer and signalled Tony for another one.

Damn woman's not going to get the better of me.

Tessa's chest tightened, semi-conscious of Blake's gaze intermittingly crossing to her. Focussed on Sophie's hilarious tales, she wiped a runaway tear from her eye. It felt good, damn good, to laugh. Sophie's detailed explanation of her daily routine with three-year-old twins had Tessa in stitches of laughter. She'd wished she had seen them when they'd demolished Tony's Christmas tree in the corner of the grill, the very same day he'd set it up. She'd been away too long, it was just like old times, as if she'd never left. A twinge of regret pitted itself in the bottom of Tessa's stomach.

"So, are you going to the reunion?" Sophie asked, bright-eyed.

Tessa's gut clenched. "Um, I'm not sure. Maybe."

"You have to go, it's Christmas and we all know you love that time of year. Everyone is going to want to hear about your life in London," Sophie said.

"I'm not really sure there's much to tell."

Sophie's frowned. "What do you mean *there's not much to tell?* In your last letter, you said things were going, what was it you said...oh that's right, things were going smashingly."

A crimson blush spread across Tessa's face and neck. *Oh God, this is going to be harder than I thought.*

"Tessa?" Sophie's voice deepened. "You're blushing. You never blush, unless you're hiding something."

Damn it, she was never good at hiding things from Sophie. Tessa's eyes widened. "Um, well..." She swallowed hard, her heart racing inside her chest like a freight train out of control.

"Tessa, tell me. What's wrong," Sophie asked, her voice edged with concern.

Nervous tension ricocheted up Tessa's spine. "Well, actually, things haven't gone exactly as I'd hoped."

"But you said in your letter that things were going well."

"I know," —she paused and her heart sped up— "and things are going well, just not in the way you think."

"What are you talking about?"

Tessa rubbed her sweaty palms down her jeans. "Sophie, I work in a delicatessen, it was the only steady full-time job I could get, and teach drama part time."

Sophie's face whitened. "You work in a what? I...I don't understand."

"It was tough, tougher than I ever thought possible. Here I was, thinking I was this great actor and I'd be able to waltz in and become this sought-after, amazing leading lady, when really I couldn't hold a candle to any of them." Her throat knotted until she could barely breathe. "I totally sucked, but I couldn't tell you what a complete failure I was. I was so embarrassed. I couldn't come back after the awful way I behaved before I left."

Sophie stared at her with an open mouth. She opened and closed it several times but nothing came out. The tense silence between them dragged on longer than Tessa had feared. Then Sophie's entire expression softened. "I'm not happy you didn't confide in me. You could have told me, I would have understood."

Relief made her weak. Thank God she was sitting down or she may have fallen down. Sophie smiled and the depth of emotion in her eyes blew Tessa away.

"Sophie, promise me you won't say anything?" she begged.

"I'm sure people will understand," Sophie said.

"Maybe, but until I've had a chance to come clean with my mum, I'd rather she hear it from me, rather than from the town gossip train." Tessa held her breath, her chest tightening under the pressure.

Sophie's frowned. "All right, but don't take too long."

Tessa nodded and let her breath out in a whoosh that made her light-headed.

Sophie's eyes thinned. "So, what about your love life, any luck there?"

Tessa shrugged. "I've had a few, but nothing serious."

"Neither has Blake," Sophie said.

Tessa's whole body froze at the mention of Blake's name. *Oh, no. Sophie please don't say it.*

Sophie continued, oblivious to the hurt and pain embedded deep in Tessa's eyes. "He hasn't had a steady girlfriend since you left, you know. All of a sudden, you were on a plane to London and you never did tell me the complete story about why you two really broke up, but now that you're back in town—"

Don't say it.

"Maybe you two can—"

She said it.

"That ship has sailed, Sophie," Tessa cut in. "I've moved on and I'm sure he has too." Pain crept over her heart as she stole a glance in his direction. She whipped her hands under the table as they began to shake. *Why is it he still looks good enough to eat and I feel as if I've aged twenty years? It's as if the last six years never affected him at all.*

His cargo pants hugged his backside like a glove. Her hands twitched, eager to glide over his toned shoulders. Even after all this time, just being in the same room as him still affected her the way it had when they first met.

Well, not any more, she thought.

Tessa cleared her throat. "Well, I wasn't going to say anything, but I have met someone since I've been back."

"What?" Sophie gasped.

"I'm not sure it will go anywhere." Tessa swallowed. Her heart pounded in her chest. *I'm going straight to hell. They may as well lock me up now and throw away the key.* She quickly continued. "He's different, really nice and easy to talk to."

Sophie finished up the last of her Christmas pudding and shuffled forward in her seat. "Oh, my God, tell me. I want to know everything." The buzz of Sophie's mobile vibrated it across the table. She sighed and answered the phone, motioning Tessa to pause mid-sentence. "Sophie Swanstone, here…are you serious…no, no don't do anything, I'm on my way."

Relief swarmed Tessa's body.

"Damn it. That was the day care. Robbie's taken a tumble and although they said it wasn't too bad, I really should take him to get checked out," Sophie said moving to stand. "This conversation is far from over, young lady. Now, come here and give me a hug."

Tessa knew she dodged a bullet on that one. Hugging Sophie goodbye, she breathed a sigh of relief and watched Sophie's flowy red curls sway as she walked out the door. Tessa flopped her elbows on the table and dropped her head into her hands.

She curled her fingers through her hair. "Could this day get any worse?" she mumbled. Turning to leave, her stomach bottomed out at the sight of Blake's robust figure still perched on the bar stool.

Yes, looks like it can. No problem, I'll just sit here and pretend to sip my coffee from my empty cup until he leaves.

She gazed around at the gatherings of people happily eating their lunch. She always remembered it being busy, but never this busy and, with so many families now buzzing with the festive season vibe. Jovial laughter filled the air, while Christmas carols played in the background. She's attracted a few side-ways glances from different people and she consciously ignored them, her eye focussed on her empty cup.

She took another fake sip. *This is ridiculous.* Even though she hadn't had a job in a while, she was still a good actor. If there's one role she could play well, it was the snubbed lover. If she kept her head down, he probably wouldn't even notice her.

She took a deep breath and glanced towards the door. Their gazes connected for a moment and his brown eyes flickered. A hint of reaction in their depths. He turned, swallowed a gulp of his beer and continued his conversation with Tony.

She shuddered, and she held her hands tight together to stop their shaking, furious at her lack of control. Who was she kidding? She willed herself to remain calm and not outwardly react to the murmurs around her.

Tessa tensed against the seat. Her palms grew sweatier by the minute. Movement at the bar nabbed her attention. Blake was finally leaving and not a moment too soon. She wasn't sure how much longer she would be able to sit, enduring the mounting stares of those that passed her.

Realising Blake had gone, a sigh of relief brushed over her. Finally, she could get back to the hospital and pray the doctor hadn't made his rounds yet. Heading out of Tony's, her mind preoccupied with the list of questions for the doctor, she totally missed the tall, robust hunk of muscle heading straight towards her.

"Excuse me. It would help if you…" She trailed off, raising her eyes from the broken pavement. Two beautiful dark russet-brown eyes bore into her soul. Her voice dropped to a whisper. "Looked where you were going."

"I'm sorry," Blake barked out a laugh. "It wasn't my intention to bowl you over." He ran his hand through his hair, staring at Tessa.

She swallowed, his eyes held hers in a trance. "No, of course not." She hadn't been this close to him in six years, but in two seconds flat, she was transported back to the past like a speeding bullet. She was utterly numb and unprepared for the adrenaline that soared through her veins.

"Tessa, how nice to see you again."

Nice? Nice to see me?

"I heard you were back in town," he said.

She blinked her eyes a few times, breaking his spell. *Focus.* "I'm sure you did. News always did travel fast in this town."

Blake's eyes drilled intently into hers. His voice grew serious. "I'm really sorry to hear about your mum and that she's been hospitalised. I knew she wasn't well but I didn't know how serious it was."

She smiled. "Thank you. I wasn't aware of it, myself."

"Well, maybe if you visited her once in a while, you might know more," he growled.

She paled, his words stabbing a gigantic hole in her heart. She knew she was a terrible daughter, what right did he have to rub it in?

He must have sensed her withdrawal. "But then again, you have been working on your career. Your mum keeps telling everyone how proud she is."

Oh God, please stop. Nausea erupted in the pit of her stomach. Tessa wanted to scream until her lungs were void of air. Scream at him for her failed career, scream at him for dumping her and scream at him for not following her to London like he promised he would.

"Thank you for your concern, Blake," she said, taking a step back. "You're right, I should have visited more, but my career is important to me."

Blake's eyes darkened to black, like an approaching thunderstorm. "Yeah, I remember."

How can he stand there as if I was the one that destroyed everything, not the other way around? She would have given up her career for this man, all he'd had to do was ask. Instead, he'd walked away from her, ripping her heart out in the process.

Enough about my disastrous life.

She cleared her throat. "Surely, you have better things to do with your time, like work, for instance?"

The corner of his lips turned up into a smile. "Yes, I do. I actually took over my dad's real estate business."

"Really?"

He frowned, crossed his arms and puffed out his chest. "What's that supposed to mean?"

"Nothing, I just didn't know, that's all. I thought you were dead-set on being an architect?" she said.

Sudden realisation dawned on his face. "You really don't know what's been happening around here, do you?"

She shook her head.

"After I did one year at University, I decided architecture wasn't for me. Until I decided what I wanted to do, I helped Dad out in the business and realised I was really good at it. When he retired, I bought the business from him." His eyes beamed with pride and for some reason, her eyes were drawn to his luscious lips. "Now, I've expanded to eleven real estate agencies. Two here in town, and the rest in surrounding towns."

His voice bled through her veins. She fought the betraying flush that slowly crept up her neck.

Well, at least one of us has made a success of themselves.

"That's really great. I'm happy for you." *Escape.* She wasn't going to hold it together much longer. "Listen, it was good to see you again, but I should get to the hospital."

He nodded. "Of course."

She backed up a few steps and smiled. His voice froze her to the spot. "Are you going to the Christmas reunion on Saturday?"

Her breath caught in her throat and tears stung her eyes. She held them back, refusing to cry over this man again. "No, I'm sorry I don't think I will be able to attend." His eyes narrowed and she refused to let him guilt her into attending. "Please let everyone know I said hello."

"I won't be going either," he snarled. "I couldn't think of anything worse than having my past thrown in my face. But I thought you might at least attend to show a little interest in the people that helped support your career in the beginning."

"It was tough trying to build a career from the ground up. Surely you, of all people, can understand that?"

"I might, but what about your mother?" he snapped.

She gasped. "What about my mother?"

"Don't you think it's about time you dealt with her illness? Wake up, Tessa she isn't going to be around forever."

She paled and began to tremble, her angry eyes glared at him. "Don't you *dare* talk to me about my mother. You know nothing about her, or me, for that matter, so why don't you keep your opinions to yourself and leave my mother to me?"

"Typical." He glared angry daggers at her. "Always thinking about yourself and your career. You were selfish back then, and you're selfish now. I guess nothing's changed."

She stared open mouthed at his outburst. "Selfish?"

"Yeah, selfish. Your career came first, stuff anyone else who cared about you and what they wanted." He turned his back on her. "So long, Tessa. Have a nice life."

Rage hurled through her veins. She couldn't control the flex of her fingers into fists. She could swear people were staring at her. Her jaw clenched and she wanted nothing more than to follow Blake and sock him one in the nose. But she wouldn't give him the satisfaction of showing how much his words had affected her.

Selfish...Selfish, ha? He has the audacity to call me selfish. Tessa's body shook. She turned on her heel and made a beeline for her car. She took several deep breaths and whispered positive, calming affirmations to herself. By the time she arrived at the hospital, she'd managed to hide her hurt from roving eyes.

Easing the door open, Tessa spotted her mother resting comfortably in her bed. "Afternoon, Mum," she said, closing the door behind her.

Lyndall's eyes squinted focusing on Tessa's frame. A spark of recognition ignited a warm smile on her lips. "Tessa? Is it really you?"

"Yes, Mum. It's really me. I came back to spend Christmas with you." she said, engulfing her in a much-needed hug.

"They said you'd popped in, but I didn't believe them," she said, her voice a little hoarse. "I said, 'Not my Tessa, she's a movie star.'"

Tessa shook her head. "No, Mum. I perform on stage in a theatre, you're the movie star... Remember?"

Lyndall's face fell, as if her whole world had just collapsed. "Oh...I'm a movie star?"

"That's right. A great movie star." *If only I could be half as good as you were.*

Tears welled in Lyndall's eyes. "When? I don't remember."

Tessa's chest ached. She'd grown up with a strong-willed, determined woman, not this frail woman, wasting away to a deliberating disease robbing her of mind and body. "A long time ago, when you were in your twenties. You starred in movies, mostly romance. You were an amazing actress, Mum. You're one of the reasons I went into acting."

"I was?" she whispered.

She nodded. "Yes, but I could never be as good as you." *Or so they tell me.*

Her eyes lit up like a beacon. "London. I remember you went to London."

Tessa's gut churned. *Of course, she would remember the day I ruined my life.*

'But you were in love with Blake?"

Her mother hadn't spoken of Blake since the day he'd walked out on Tessa. She'd banned his name from her house. Why bring it up now? "Yes, I *was* in love with Blake, but I chose to go London to be a star like you."

"And are you?"

She fought the urge to colour the truth. It wouldn't matter, she probably wouldn't remember if she told her anyway. "No, no, Mum, I'm not. I tried but I just couldn't score the roles like you did. I guess I just don't have the X factor most directors are looking for."

"You left Blake behind?" she asked.

"No, Mum," she sighed, frustration setting in. "I didn't leave Blake behind...he left me, remember?"

"Yes...yes I do remember." Lyndall closed her eyes, the energy of conversation taking its toll. "I'm sorry, Tessa. So, very sorry. I was wrong."

She frowned and stared at her mother in complete bewilderment, shock bleeding up her spine. Tessa had never heard her mother apologise—to anyone, let alone, admit she was wrong. *Wrong about what?*

"It's okay, Mum. Don't worry, I've got everything under control. Just rest."

She nodded, resting her head back against the soft feather pillow. Tessa pulled the white, knitted blanket up around her mother's shoulders and tucked her in. Tessa sat staring at her mother's frown, trying to understand why she'd apologised.

Light murmurs from the bed, startled Tessa from her thoughts. "Wrong...letter...Tessa, no."

"Shhh, Mum," Tessa said easing from her chair to the bed. She gently stroked Lyndall's hair away from her sweaty forehead, calming her while she slept. "Shh, Mum. It's all right, Tessa's home, now," she repeated. Lyndall's heavy breathing filled the quiet room, signalling she'd succumbed to a deep sleep.

"Tessa," Isaac's voice rang out from the door. "How nice to see you again."

"Hi, Isaac," Tessa said softly, nodding in his direction.

"Just giving you a head's up, the doctor's making rounds now. So, he should be here in the next ten or so minutes."

Thank goodness, she thought.

"Thanks. I'll be here."

He smiled. "I've got a few more patients to see and then I'll pop back for a chat, if you're up for it?"

"Sure. Sounds great."

Tessa jumped when the door swung open no less than five minutes after Isaac left. She gasped and her hand flew to her chest.

"I'm sorry, Tessa, I didn't mean to startle you," Doctor Lawson said, moving to shake her hand.

"No, that's fine. I was just off with the fairies so to speak." she said with a chuckle.

His brow creased as he looked at Lyndall. "I think it would be better if we talked outside."

A cold shiver ran up her spine. "Sure." Tessa swallowed the lump in her throat as she closed the door behind her.

He looked at her with a stern look embedded on his features. "Did you do the research on Dementia like I asked you to when we first spoke?"

Damn it. "Um, no I haven't gotten around to it yet."

He sighed. "I think it's important to understand what this disease does to the mind and body and how it's going to affect your mother in the future."

"I know. I will and then we can discuss where to go from here."

He pointed to the pair of seats in the corridor. "There's no time like the present. Why don't we take a seat?"

Tessa forced her feet to move even though they felt like lead weights strapped to the floor.

"Your mum has been struggling for a while now, both with the dementia and also her general health. She refused to tell you the truth, because she didn't want to worry you."

Struggling?

"We're just damn lucky that it was Pastor Steve's day to visit, otherwise we may not have found her in time. The only reason she's in the hospital now is because Steve insisted on it or he would call an ambulance and then the whole town would know. That's why I asked him to call you in London. I thought it was important for you to be aware of the gravity of her situation."

Tessa gasped. "She said nothing to me."

"Well, she wouldn't, would she?" he said leaning forward, his elbows resting on his knees. "Let's face it, Tessa you haven't really been a prominent figure in her life for some time, which is not your fault by any means. It's hard to start out in a new career and it can be time consuming."

Guilt hung dark over her heart. His brow furrowed and her heart plummeted.

"But her going home by herself isn't an option anymore, and I'm not sure you're ready to become a full-time care-giver, which is what she's going to need."

The sudden realisation of his words dawned on her. Guilt, grief and pain crept through her like wildfire. "So, what are you saying…really?"

His tone was heavy. "I'm saying that she won't be able to go home without someone with the medical knowledge to care for her. She's going to need constant care, especially when the disease becomes more debilitating. It's something you're going to have to think about very seriously."

She nodded. Sadness crept over her as she realised her fate. This was her mother, they may not have always got on, but she was still her mother and she loved her.

"Thank you, Doctor Lawson. I hear what you're saying and I'll take care of it."

He smiled and placed a comforting hand on her shoulder. "I'm sure you will. Do some reading on the progression of dementia. It will inform you of what you can expect in the future. If you have any questions, don't hesitate to ask."

Anxiety began to root itself in the pit of her stomach. "I will. Thank you." She watched as he moved down the hall to the nurse's station.

She closed her eyes and propped her head against the wall. *If only I hadn't been so obsessed with my career, maybe I would have seen beyond her façade.* To do that, she would have had to return home; broke, jobless and boyfriendless.

"Penny for your thoughts," Isaac said as he sat down on the chair beside her.

For the longest time, she just sat there next to Isaac, silent, letting Doctor Lawson's words sink in.

"So, I guess the doctor explained things, huh?" he said.

She nodded. "Yeah, he did."

"Does that mean you'll be moving back to Whittaker Springs for good?"

She froze, dread snaked up her spine. How could she move back to Whittaker Springs, permanently? "I'm not sure." She said with a heavy heart. *God, after what happened with Blake this afternoon, how could I possibly come back, now?*

The responsibility now fell to her to take care of her mother, but not in Whittaker Springs. She'd find a good care facility, maybe in Vermont, that could look after Lyndall and a teaching job close by.

A knot formed in her throat. Her mind made up she turned to Isaac. "No, I won't be coming back to Whittaker Springs." *There is nothing to really hold me here, anymore.* "I'll need to look for a place in a more established town that will cater to Mum's medical needs. That way I can also try and get some work."

"Really," Isaac said with raised eyebrows. "What about Blake?"

The breath squeezed from her lungs and she sucked in much needed air. "Blake and I are over, have been over for a long time. He's moved on and so have I."

"That's not what I hear on the town grapevine," he chuckled.

Tessa flew from her chair, her hands thrust sharply on her hips. "What are you talking about?"

Isaac jumped up as if his pants were on fire. "Well, rumour has it, since your so-called discussion with Blake outside Tony's Bar and Grill, he's decided that dating is not for him. He dumped his on-again, off-again girlfriend—for good, this time—and announced he is boycotting the reunion tomorrow night."

Her brow creased. "Where did you hear that?"

"Glad you asked. I was in Pastry Plus Café today, placing my Christmas order, and I just happened to overhear a few ladies talking. Isn't it obvious? He's still in love with you. That's why he dumped the last girl he was casually seeing and that's why he's not going to the reunion. Because it reminds him of you."

Her mouth went dry and tears threatened. She swallowed the growing knot in her throat. "Oh, for God's sake, Isaac." In a swift move, she headed back into her mother's room, hoping he wouldn't follow.

That can't be true, can it? Cold fingers of dread gripped her heart. Blake will always be the one that got away. She'd never love another the way she loved Blake. She'd closed her heart to love a long time ago. Even if she did still love

Blake, it wasn't worth the risk of destroying her heart forever.

Isaac's voice echoed through the room. "So, if he's not going to the reunion, you can."

Her eyes widened in alarm. "Ah, I don't think so. That's the last thing I want to do. My focus now is on finding my mother a top-notch place, where she'll be looked after, and sorting out her house. The sooner I do that, the sooner I can leave this town."

"Hey," Isaac said thrusting his hand across his wounded heart. "Ease up, that's my new home you're talking about."

The tension eased from Tessa's body. She chuckled, shaking her head. "You're right. I'm sorry."

A shallow voice barely caught her attention. "Tessa, is that you?"

Tessa's eyes widened and her head whipped around. "Yes, Mum, it's me," she said clasping her mother's hand in hers. She softly ran her fingers over the back of mother's palm, her thin, wrinkled skin showing her age.

"The letters," Lyndall whispered. "You need to read the letters."

"Letters?"

"The letters," she muttered.

"What letters, Mum?

She sighed and closed her eyes. "The letters."

"Okay, I'll read the letters." She gazed at Isaac and he shook his head puzzled by her words.

"I'll pop back and see you tomorrow." Tessa sucked in her breath, sorrow washing into her eyes. A loan tear rolled down Tessa's cheek. She wiped it away with the back of her hand, her eyes fixated on the steady rise and fall of her mother's chest.

"I'm sorry, Tessa. I didn't mean to upset you," Isaac said moving further into the room. "I should know better than to listen to idle gossip, especially where love is concerned."

She shook her head. "It's all right."

He groaned, a look of disappointment strewn across his face. "I just thought that since Blake wasn't going to the reunion, it would be a great opportunity for you to go without the prospect of running into him." He raised his eyebrows. "Since you're leaving town anyway, what's the harm in going along and having a little fun with your old schoolmates? You could let your hair down a little, not to mention, you'll be able to introduce me to some locals. What do you say?" She couldn't help but laugh when he flashed his emerald eyes at her.

"All right," she chuckled. The warmth from his smile bled into her heart. "You've convinced me. Pick me up at seven." She picked up her bag, kissed her mother goodbye and headed for the door.

"You won't regret it," he said.

"Shh." She glared at him, her pointer finger covering her puckered lips.

He shrugged. "Oops, sorry. It's just…since moving to Whittaker Springs, this will be my first real night out that doesn't involve walking down the street to pick up one of Gordo's pizzas. I'm itching to spread my wings."

Tessa scowled and rolled her eyes. "Come on, walk me out and we'll talk details."

Chapter Three

BLAKE PACED THE confines of his office, anger knotting the insides of his stomach. A soft breeze blew and light snow fell outside the window. The room was ablaze with warmth from the fire, but Blake's heart felt as cold as the frigid air outside. He was so damn mad at Tessa, he was very close to losing it altogether. He glanced at the files on his desk. "What the hell am I doing at work on a Saturday afternoon?" He never worked Saturdays, but sitting at home wasn't helping either. Yesterday's public argument with Tessa played out in his head like a broken record.

That woman had the audacity to stroll back into town and play the innocent victim. Her selfishness astounded him. His jaw clenched and he wanted nothing more than to wipe the woman from his mind. *Permanently.*

Setting eyes on her again bombarded him with so many conflicting emotions that it unsteadied him. He wished she'd stayed away for good. She looked as gorgeous yesterday as the first day they'd met. Trust her to come back in to town and crush the festive joy out of him.

His skin prickled and nausea welled in his stomach. Their last soul-destroying conversation, six years ago, rooted in his mind forever.

Hearing the truth from her mother about Tessa's true motives destroyed him that day. She'd been too selfish to tell him herself. Thank God, her mother had the decency to, before he'd made a total fool of himself.

He'd been blindsided like a lovesick fool. If only he'd realised sooner that her love for him was fake, a ploy to string him along while she made it big and then publicly dump him for all the world to see.

Blake's expression darkened. "Well, you may have pulled the wool over my eyes once, I can promise you it will never happen again." If he set eyes on her again it would be too soon.

Blake busied himself with the Shaw rental file when his office line buzzed. "Blake Bryant." He leant back in his chair and rolled his eyes as Kelly's high-pitched squeal assaulted his ears. *Great, just what I need, the town know-it-all.* "Kelly, what can I do for you?"

"Blake, thank goodness I tracked you down. We've got a major problem," Kelly said breathlessly.

"What are you talking about?"

"Adam was supposed to give the speech tonight but has broken out in the chicken pox and won't be able to make it, so you're it."

"I'm what?" he asked taking a sip of his cold coffee.

"You'll have to step up and give the speech."

He coughed and spluttered, unsure if it was Kelly's words or the stone-cold coffee that blocked his airway. Over his dead body. "Listen, Kelly, you're going to have to find someone else. Things have changed…I won't be going to the reunion tonight, after all."

"What are you talking about," she blurted out. "You have to go. Everyone is counting on it. You have a reputation to uphold, one of honour and commitment, and now that Adam's not well enough to speak, you have to do it, you just have to." Why the hell they decided to combine their ten-year school reunion with Christmas, he'd never know.

The idea froze his blood. Ten years ago, when they'd left school, he'd been the happiest man alive. He'd had his future planned. A life supporting Tessa's dream in London, then back to Whittaker Springs to settle down and have a family, or so he thought.

Inwardly, he winced. Be damn if he was going to get up in front of his long-time high school buddies and pretend he was living the life he dreamed of. Tessa single-handedly destroyed that dream. Why put himself in the firing line of pity and ridicule?

"Kelly, I said it before and I'll say it again, I'm not going to the reunion. You'll have to find someone else to give the speech."

"I can't believe you would do this to me, Blake, and at Christmas time. You know how hard I've worked on making this the best Christmas party ever. Where is your community spirit?" she snapped. "You're obviously not the man I thought you were."

The thud of the phone slamming down reverberated in his ear.

He tensed. The thought of a mere glimpse of Tessa, dressed to the nines and looking as beautiful as she did ten years ago, sent shivers up his spine. "What is it about you Tessa that gets me so riled up?"

"Because you're still in love with her, always have been, always will be."

Blake spun a one-eighty to see his dad propped up against the doorframe, his winter coat covered in a light dusting of fresh snow and his arms folded across his chest. A smug smile spread across his face.

Blake felt the blood drain from his face. "What are you talking about?"

"You were never the same after she left. Son, your heart's been with Tessa all this time."

He shook his head and rage flooded his veins. "No, you're wrong. I don't love her. I may have once, that was until she walked out on *me*. She threw *my* love back in my face."

"That may be so, but you also haven't had any long-term relationships or fallen in love since Tessa. Why do you think that is?"

He didn't want to think about it. An invisible hand crushed his chest, draining the air from his lungs. "I get it, Dad. You and Mum want grandkids—"

"Jesus, Blake. You think this is about grandkids?" he snapped. "Sure, your mother and I want them before we're too old to enjoy them, but this is about you being happy. And Tessa made you happy. That's all your mother and I really want, son."

He stared open mouthed at his father.

"Now, about the reunion tonight," he said rubbing his chin. "You're a fine upstanding member of our community. Since when do you not follow through with a commitment you've made? We brought you up better that. You were going yesterday, dare I ask what's changed?"

Blake sighed. "I think you know what's changed, Dad."

"So, be the man I raised. The one that faces challenges head on, instead of one that cowers behind his office desk."

Why do you always have to be right?

"I heard about your heated discussion with Tessa, outside Tony's yesterday. Go tonight and make it right with her. She'll have enough to worry about with her mother, now that she needs constant care."

"She won't be there," Blake said. "But you're right. I said I would go and Bryants are always true to their word. Thanks, Dad." He rubbed his forehead with his hand and sighed. "I'll call Kelly back."

He smiled. "And while you're at it, why not call Tessa and make a time to see her. Talk to her, find out what really happened all those years ago."

"I'm not sure that would be such a good idea."

His dad turned toward the door and paused, pulling his beanie over his semi-balding head. "You never know unless you try, son."

Blake's pulse raced and his heart pounded inside his chest. He wasn't sure how Tessa would react to seeing him again. He wasn't sure how he would handle it. If he did confront her, at least he would know the real reason she'd lied to him all those years ago. He remembered her saying she wasn't going to the reunion. What harm would it do if he stopped by her house on his way?

※ ※ ※

Blake gripped the steering wheel with whitened knuckles as his car neared Tessa's house. His heart raced. He was surprised it didn't burst right out of his chest.

What would he say, when he was finally standing face to face with her again? *Oh, hi, Tessa, want to tell me why you decided to throw away our love when I was perfectly happy to follow you around the world like a sick puppy dog?* He chuckled. *Like that's going to work.*

Blake noticed Tessa's house was the only one in the street without Christmas lights. Guilt stabbed at his heart. Everyone knew Lyndall's health was deteriorating. *I should have made more of an effort to help her see in the Christmas season.*

He eased off the gas, ready to pull his car into Tessa's driveway. He hesitated when movement on her porch caught his eye. He froze. *What the hell?* Fury ran hot in his veins. Here he was, ready to let her back into his heart, when she had already given hers to someone else. Watching her fly into the arms of another man crushed him.

Tessa's smile beamed from one ear to the other as he twirled her around. Anger rose inside his chest 'til he thought it would consume every last breath he possessed.

"What a complete fucking idiot I am?"

He swerved the car back onto the road and prayed she hadn't noticed the disastrous mistake he almost made…again. "That's it, no more," his eyes blazed with anger. "She can go to hell as far as I'm concerned. In fact, all women can go to hell." He'd go to the reunion, do the speech and then skip out on the rest.

❄ ❄ ❄

"Sweet mother of God," Isaac uttered under his breath as his wide eyes roamed up and down her slender body.

Tessa grinned. "So, you like it?" she asked twirling around. "You don't think it's too much, do you?"

"Like it? I absolutely love it and it's totally gorgeous on you. Definitely not too much. As a matter of fact, I'd say it is the perfect outfit for a Christmas event. Just the right shade of ruby red and enough bling to make you sparkle."

Tessa threw her head back and laughed. Her chest buzzed with warmth. It felt good to laugh, something she hadn't done enough of lately.

"Where on earth did you find this gem?" he said holding her hands out wide to examine her exquisite princess-line dress.

"Actually, in my mum's wardrobe. If we're going to move, I thought it'd be as good a time as any to clean out her clothes."

"Listen, speaking of moving, I hope you don't mind, but I made a few calls for you and I managed to find a bed for your mother at Yarra Pines Care Facility, in Burlington. It has an amazing reputation and is one of the best in the city."

She gasped, and her hand flew to her throat. "What?"

"I'm not sure if you were planning on moving that far away from Whittaker Springs, but they provide the best care by a long shot. It's not a done deal, by any means. You need to meet the manager and get through the interview. I just got you a foot in the door, that's all," he said flinging his hand as if it was nothing.

"Oh, my God. Thank you. I don't care where it is as long as Mum has the best care," she said as she flung her arms tight around his neck. "Thank you, thank you, thank you."

She kept repeating it, not giving a second thought to breathing. Tessa soaked up Isaac's comforting arms wrapped tightly around her waist. He spun her around, his laughter mixed with her soft voice was magic to her ears.

Isaac finally stopped spinning and planted her feet firmly on the ground. "What do you say we hit this reunion of yours?"

She'd forgotten what it was like to feel happy. "Let's do this." She smiled and headed back inside to grab her winter coat. "I'll just grab my purse and lock up."

Pulling out of the curb, Isaac drove cautiously along the icy street. He cleared his throat. "Do you mind me asking what happened with Blake?"

Isaac's question was like a punch to her stomach and for a moment she sat there like an idiot, wishing the seat would open up and swallow her, just so she wouldn't have to answer.

"I didn't mean to pry, it's just a people have been talking and I thought I'd get it straight from you, rather than listen to idle gossip."

She closed her eyes for a brief moment and then squared her shoulders. "Okay, tell me. I'd like to hear what the rumour mill has to say."

"Are you sure?"

"Why not? Best I be prepared for the onslaught of looks I'll get tonight," she snapped.

He kept his eyes glued to the road. "I heard you and Blake were an item in high school and you were set to get married. Apparently, he wanted you to stay here and have his babies, but you told him you couldn't have children and that you wouldn't let a man come between you and your career. So, you dumped him and left town to find fame and fortune in London."

Tessa stared at him, dumbfounded. Her pulse was pounding in her head. *Couldn't have children...I dumped him? Where the hell do people get their information from around here, the back of a Corn Flakes packet?*

At first, she stiffened, ready to tackle the rumours head on. But after a moment, she remembered they were just rumours and to get all worked up over the false allegations just wasn't worth it. She knew the truth. Blake broke her heart, not the other way around.

"Wow, you weren't kidding when you said you heard people talking." She paused calmly. "You shouldn't believe everything you hear, especially around this town. Things are not always what they seem."

"So, what really happened?"

Keep to the facts, Tessa.

She shrugged. "It's simple, really. I wanted to travel to London to study and become an actress and he wanted to stay here in Whittaker Springs."

"So, did you dump him or did he dump you?"

Tears stung her eyelids and she turned away. "It really doesn't matter now. It was a long time ago."

"You're right. The past is the past, and there's no use crying over what you can't change."

As the school gymnasium came into clear view, the knots in Tessa's stomach doubled. "I'm not sure this was such a good idea."

"What are you talking about?"

Her hands began to shake. She gripped them together in her lap so he wouldn't see. "Don't you get it? The rumour mill has started and God only know what other people are saying about me. Apart from the fiasco with Blake, they're all going to want to know about my great life as an actor in London. It will be humiliating telling everyone that I bombed on stage and the closest I now come to the stage is teaching Drama to little kids."

"Hey, drama happened to be one of my favourite classes when I was in school. What other class can you get up on stage and pretty much make a total fool of yourself and get great marks doing it? Drama teachers rock," he said, keeping his eyes on the road.

She laughed at his quirky view. "I know, but it isn't exactly what I bragged about doing when I left."

He turned the car into a free parking spot. "Well, just don't tell them. The way I see it, what they don't know won't hurt them."

Her brow creased. "What?"

"You're leaving town anyway, so what's the harm in keeping it a secret a little longer? When you're gone, they'll be none the wiser." He shrugged. "Problem solved and I'll be by your side the whole night, just in case you need a quick escape."

Could it really be that simple?

Tears welled in her eyes. She couldn't remember the last time someone was willing to go out on a limb for her. Isaac had wormed his way into her cold heart in the short time she'd known him.

"Oh, no, you don't," he said shaking a finger in Tessa's direction. "There will be absolutely no crying tonight. I refuse to be seen with a woman who looks like she's been punched in the face."

The warmth from his words soared through her body and she couldn't hold back the eruption of laughter that filled the car. "Okay, I'm sorry." She sniffed. "I wouldn't want to impose that kind of embarrassment on you, especially your first real night on the town."

He sighed. "Thank heavens. Now can we go and have some fun, please?"

She could no more deny his pouty puppy dog face, than she could a real puppy. "All right, let's go."

Her stomach was doing somersaults. Nervous energy bolted up her spine as she pulled her coat tight over her chest. She threaded her arm through Isaac's, took a deep breath and headed towards the gymnasium.

Reality hit her like a cold smack in the face. If she walked in on Isaac's arm right now, she knew exactly what people would think. Her heart plummeted. More snide remarks would surely fly from gawking onlookers.

Gee, it didn't take her long before she made a move on the new guy in town. What about Blake? How could she treat him so badly?

The blood pumped through her veins. "I can't do this. I'm sorry, Isaac, I can't go in there with you." She pushed away from him ready to escape the impending humiliation ahead.

"What are you talking about, you look amazing," Isaac said.

"No, no, no," she repeated, shaking her head.

"Tessa, it's all right," he said calmly.

Her heart jumped into her throat and she shook her head frantically. "No, no, it's not. You don't get it. They're all going to look at me like I'm some tramp, a cheap tart and they're all going want to know what I'm doing dating a man like you."

She was talking crap, but she couldn't stop the dribble coming out of her mouth.

Isaac's hands flew to her shoulders. "Tessa, stop right now."

Tessa's chest burned as she drew in deep breaths, filling her starved lungs with chilled air.

"You don't need to worry, Tessa. You and I will know the truth, and the truth is, that you and I can never be a couple."

His words cut deep. Had she misread his signals?

"Excuse me?" she said with a raised eyebrow.

"This is not the way I wanted to tell you, but I suppose there's no time like the present."

Frustration rooted itself in her belly. "What are you talking about?"

"Tessa…I'm gay."

She felt the blood drain from her face. Her head swam recapping their earlier conversations. *How the hell did I miss the clues?* Her voice quivered with embarrassment. "Gay," she whispered.

"Tessa?"

She paused, her cheeks burned with humiliation. Tessa's eye caught Isaac's sympathetic smile.

"It's all right," he said. "How could you have possibly known? I haven't told anyone. Like you, I've only been in town a short while, and I really didn't want to play into the typical male gay nurse stereotype, but I can't help the way I am. Speaking from experience, I know that coming out and announcing, 'I'm gay' hasn't really done me any favours."

"No, I can't imagine it has."

"But if it's any conciliation, if I were straight, I would definitely ask you out without a second thought." He said with a sweet smirk on his face.

She smiled. "You're sweet, but I'm not really girlfriend material at the moment."

He reared back. "What the hell are you talking about? You're stunning and stacked in all the right places, not to mention a great conversationalist."

"Ha," she laughed. "That will be enough flattery out of you, thank you very much."

"That's better. Now, what do you say, we stop freezing our asses off out here, and go in there and have a great night? If anyone has any issues, they can go and take a long walk off a short pier." He laughed and held his hand out palm up waiting for her acceptance.

Tessa's heart filled with gratitude. She smiled. "Sounds like a plan."

As soon as she stepped inside the building, all the breath squeezed painfully from her lungs. Everywhere she looked, her eyes fell on white and blue decorations, snowflakes, fake snow and white Christmas trees. Memories of her high school Senior Christmas dance flashed before her eyes.

Why did they have to decorate it in Winter Wonderland? Her mouth went dry and tears threatened to destroy her make-up right there on the spot. Isaac immediately sensed her unease.

"Are you all right?" he whispered in her ear.

She nodded swallowing the lump in her throat. "They've decorated it exactly the same as our Senior Christmas dance."

Isaac's brow furrowed. "So?"

She reached up and whispered in his ear. "It was the first time Blake told me he loved me."

Isaac made an O shape with his lips. "Let's just focus on having a good time tonight, okay?" She nodded.

She was thankful that the lights were dimmed, so it wasn't that easy to see people. It was pretty, she had to admit. She eyed the blue and white snowflake fairy lights that lit up the entire roof. It was like staring into a beautiful vision of the Milky Way on a clear starry night. *If only.*

Ever since she's walked through the door, the stares had increased. Whispers thrived at her expense. Some didn't even disguise the fact that they were gossiping about her. Each stare or insult stabbed at her heart with pinpointed precision.

"Tessa, you made it," Sophie's voice screeched from across the room.

Trust Sophie to make a big deal of her showing up. "Hi, Sophie," she said, wrapping her arms around her friend in a warm hug. "As if I would miss it. Besides, you wouldn't let me live it down if I didn't show my face."

"Damn straight, girlfriend." Sophie chuckled and raised her eyebrows when her eyes locked on Isaac.

She thrust her hand out in Isaac's direction. "Hi. I'm Sophie, Tessa's oldest friend. "

"Hi. I'm Isaac, Tessa's newest friend," he said with a slight cheeky smirk on his face.

Oh, Isaac, you would have to stir the pot, wouldn't you? Tessa thought.

Sophie's eyes widened. "Newest friend...really. Haven't I seen you around town before?" she asked.

"Not unless you've been at the hospital. I'm a nurse and haven't long transferred to Whittaker Springs Hospital."

"Really?" Sophie said.

A chuckle erupted deep in Tessa's stomach. "Isaac, would you mind getting us a drink, please?"

To her surprise, he turned and gave her a peck on the cheek. "Of course. Would you like me to take your coat as well?"

She nodded, quickly freeing herself of the woollen garment.

"Be right back," he said as he sauntered towards the coat room.

Sophie frowned, pulling Tessa to the side of the room. "Quick, while John's off sorting MC stuff, tell me everything. Who is he, where did you meet? What's he like in bed?"

Tessa gasped. "Sophie!"

"What," she said coyly, as if butter wouldn't melt in her mouth. "You know it's my duty as your best friend to look out for you and to do that, I need to know all the gritty details. Now spill."

Tessa held back tears of laughter. She regretted the wasted years away from her friend. "I've missed you so much, Sophie."

Sophie squeezed back. "I've missed you too and, now that you're back in town life is just going to get more exciting. We have so much to catch up on, but promise me you'll come 'round soon?"

Tessa didn't have the heart to tell her she wasn't staying in town much longer. "Of course."

"Now, who is Isaac and where did you meet him?" Sophie asked, a smile plastered on her face.

"Sophie, Isaac is one of my mum's nurses. He's new in town, only been here for a few weeks. I'm being a good friend and showing him around."

Sophie waited with bated breath. "And?"

A glint in Tessa's eye held Sophie's full attention. "And," she swallowed. "He's…"

"He's what? Come on, Tessa, don't keep me hanging here," Sophie grumbled.

"He's, um… Well—"

"Oh, never mind, you'll keep," she sighed impatiently. "It's pretty crummy news about Adam, don't you think?"

Tessa blinked in surprise and a blank gaze flashed momentarily across her face.

Sophie continued. "He came down with the chicken pox, so Blake's giving his speech."

She paled and her breathing sped up, as if her lungs were void of air. *Blake… Here… No, no, no he said he wasn't coming tonight.*

"Maybe it will give you two a chance to talk things out."

Talk things out... Are you completely out of your mind? Tessa wanted to scream the words at the top of her voice.

"Listen, I don't know what happened, but it's obviously made both of your miserable sods."

Miserable was an understatement. Yes, she was miserable, and it was all Bake's doing.

"You need to deal with it, so it doesn't eat away at you for the rest of your life." Sophie looked at her, sorrow etched in every part of her expression.

"Here you go," Isaac said, placing a strawberry daiquiri in Tessa's trembling hands. "While I was at the bar, I ran into two of your old classmates, Emma and Ashlyn."

Sophie huffed. "That's my cue to leave.

Isaac frowned. "No, Sophie, please don't leave on my account."

"It's okay, Isaac. Emma and Ashlyn aren't exactly on the top of my Christmas card list." Sophie winked at Tessa.

Oh, my God. Sophie please stop talking, thought Tessa.

Isaac leant in and whispered in Tessa's ear. "You didn't tell her about me, did you?"

Tessa shook her head. "Of course not, it's not my news to tell."

Sophie's eyes widened. "Tell me what?"

The corner of Isaac's mouth turned up in a grin as he gazed at Tessa. "Do you think we can trust her with our secret?"

Sophie folded her arms across her chest and pouted. "Secret? Yes, of course, you can trust me. What secret? Oh, come on, guys, you can tell me."

Isaac waited for Tessa's nod of approval and then huddled up to Sophie. He flung his arm around her shoulder. "You see... I'm gay."

Sophie's jaw dropped open. Tessa didn't know if she was more astounded that Sophie didn't know or that she didn't work it out herself. She always did say she had a sixth sense for reading people.

"I haven't exactly announced it to the town, yet, so please keep it to yourself."

"Of course." Sophie shrugged. "Who would I tell, anyway?"

Both Tessa and Isaac raised their eyebrows. "Do you really want me to answer that?" Tessa said, every word laced with sarcasm. Sophie visibly tensed and the hurt embedded in her eyes cut deep in Tessa's heart.

"I would *never* betray your trust, or yours, Isaac. You do know that, don't you?" she asked.

Shock bombarded Tessa. "Yes, I know."

"Tessa!"

Startled, Tessa turned at her name to see Emma and Ashlyn heading towards them.

Sophie groaned. "Let's talk later, okay?"

"Sure," Tessa said. Love spread through her veins as Sophie engulfed her in a sisterly hug.

Emma and Ashlyn ignored Sophie as she sauntered past them. "So, what's it like in London?" Emma pried.

"Um," Tessa mumbled.

"Are the men as gorgeous as they are in the movies?" Ashlyn added.

Emma continued. "Have you done any nude scenes with naked men?"

Isaac coughed and threw his arm around Tessa's shoulder. "Tessa and I could use some alone time," —he winked— "if you know what I mean?"

Nausea struck again. This time she could taste the bile in her mouth. Their pathetic high-pitched giggles filled Tessa's ears as they sashayed away.

Fury burned inside her chest. She threw Isaac's arm from her shoulder and glared daggers at him. "Have you lost your mind?"

He took a swig of his daiquiri. "I figured if people are going to talk, I may as well give them something to talk about."

Tessa's blood was a fire scorching through her veins. "That was *not* part of the deal, Isaac." She closed her eyes and braced herself for the inevitable battle ahead.

He frowned. "You're right. I guess I got a little carried away." Isaac placed his drink on the table. "I'm sorry."

She chuckled and caved under the pressure of his cutesy smile. "Listen, how about we call it a night? I've had enough."

He gasped as if someone had just stabbed him in the heart. "Why? If it's because of my stupid behaviour, I said I was sorry. Don't let me spoil your night. The party's just getting started."

"Blake's here." His name caught in her throat.

"Oh." Isaac paled. "I thought he wasn't coming."

"So did I, but apparently there was a change of plans." Her mouth went dry. "Let's just get out of here, please?"

"But, we haven't even had a dance yet."

"Do you really think that's wise?" Tessa said distracted by the joyful sounds bombarding her senses.

Christmas carols drummed in her ears. Hearty laughs, people greeting old faces for the first time since high school. A stab of misery shot through her heart like a knife. She'd missed out on so much when she left. The

Christmas carols vanished and Justin Timberlake's *Sexy Back* boomed through the speakers.

"Oh, my God, this is one of my favourite songs." Isaac almost jumped out of his skin. "One dance, please, please, please," he begged. "And then we'll go. Promise."

Tessa couldn't help but laugh at Isaac's bubbling energy. He was jumping around as if he had ants in his pants. "Okay, calm down. One song." Isaac grabbed her hands and weaved them into the centre of the crowded dance floor. They moved, bounded, jiggled and hip-bumped to the beat of the music until she was perspiring like a professional dancer. Laughter and warmth filled her chest.

"Mind if I cut in?" Blake's voice snapped her back to reality.

She froze, even though the beat kept pounding on around her. Panic vibrated through every single nerve ending, until she thought her entire head would explode.

Get a grip, woman. You're an actor, how about you start acting like one.

She flicked her raven-black hair over her shoulder, eyed Isaac, grabbed his arm and pulled him close. "I'm sorry, but Isaac and I were just on our last dance."

Blake's bold gaze flickered from hers to Isaac's, then to their joined arms. She could feel his jealously simmering, building, ready to explode.

His eyes narrowed. "Surely, you can spare one dance for an old school buddy. I'm sure Isaac won't mind, will you?"

Isaac grunted and hugged Tessa closer. "If Tessa minds, then so do I."

Anger started to simmer deep in her belly. The time for cowering was over. There was only one way to deal with her past and that was to tackle it head on. "That's all right, Isaac. I'll have one dance with my 'old school buddy' and then we'll head out."

Isaac caught her eye and raised an eyebrow. "Are you sure?"

She nodded, ignoring the huge knot in her stomach. "Yes, I'm sure. Why don't you wait for me by the buffet and I'll meet you there after our dance?" He nodded and moved away, giving Blake an evil glare that would rival Frankenstein.

"Blake, how nice to see you again," she said swaying her hips to the upbeat music.

"I wish I could say the same."

She stopped and recoiled at his blunt statement. "Why did you ask me to dance, if you didn't want to see me?"

"Because, Tessa, we have unfinished business," he said, his eyes boring into her soul.

Without warning, the song beat changed. Robin Thicke's voice boomed out the words to *Lost without You*. *What the hell?* Repulsion erupted in the pit of her stomach and it took every ounce of willpower not to turn and run from the gymnasium. Had he planned for their song to come on? What was he up to?

"Shall we?" He asked, holding his arms out.

Dancing with Blake was one thing, but being held in his strong arms was something completely different altogether. Her hands itched to touch him. She was wrong, so wrong. Facing up to the past was a stupid idea. Ignoring it and running away was a much better option.

"Um. Blake, I don't think that's a good idea."

He sent her a smouldering look. One that tested her willpower. "Why? Afraid?"

She sucked in a deep breath through her nostrils and held her chin up high and shook her head.

Yes.

"Afraid your boyfriend will object?" he blurted out.
Boyfriend? Oh, my God. Blake thinks Isaac's my boyfriend.

'Of course not." She held her breath and stepped into Blake's waiting embrace. Pleasure, pure pleasure, seared through her veins as her body met his. Her breathing sped up, despite her gallant attempts to appear unflustered. Their bodies moved as one. Wave after wave of desire washed over her and spread throughout her limbs, until she thought she might pass out.

How can she still want him so badly, after the way he dumped her? One song, just one song.

His eyes sought hers out. "Tell me, Tessa, will Isaac follow you back to London when you leave?"

"What?"

"When you decide to leave again, will he follow you back as I would have?" he asked, pulling her tighter against his ridged body.

"What are you talking about?" she asked in a stark voice. "You and I both know you weren't prepared to come with me. You wanted me to be the little housewife that had the dinner ready on the table when you came home from a hard day's work, and that just wasn't me."

His eyes blazed with anger. "What the hell are you talking about?"

"Oh, come off it, Blake. You couldn't stand the fact that I wanted out of this town. That I wanted to make something of myself."

"What I couldn't stand was your manipulative, lying, deceitful tactics." Blake spat.

Tears welled in her eyes. His words, cold and harsh tore through her heart.

"Yeah, that's right. I know everything," he said, vengeance tainting every word. "But pretending to be in love with me, pretending to want to have my children, was really beneath even a sexy seductress like you."

Tessa was speechless. *Sexy seductress*. Paralysed with a multitude of emotions running ramped through her body. He was blaming *her* for their breakup? Blaming her for manipulating *him*.

She shoved his hands away from her blazing body. "Me," she gasped between burning breathes. "I'm the liar? That's rich coming, from you. You didn't even have the decency to respond when I wrote you."

"You never wrote me."

"Oh, so now who's the liar," she said smugly. "Go to hell, Blake," she said, turning to find an escape.

His hands moved quicker that she did clutching her upper arm anchoring her to his body. "Tessa?"

Her skin burned under his touch. Tessa's body shook with enough anger to ignite a volcano. She withdrew her free arm and swung as hard as she could, branding her hand flat across his cheek. The force of the blow released her instantly. "Bastard," she yelled and bolted through the crowd of interested onlookers, tears streaming down her face.

Chapter Four

"OH, GOD, MUM, what a mess I've made of my life." Tessa buried her head in her hands and sobbed. "I'm a complete and utter screw-up." She leant back in the chair, grabbed another handful of tissues and blew her nose.

Her thoughts in chaos, Tessa wiped her eyes and attempted to make sense of Blake's harsh words. *Pretending to be in love with him...pretending to want to have his children...sexy seductress. I never pretended anything. I loved him more than life itself.*

Tessa spoke in soft words to her sleeping mother. "It doesn't matter, now, anyway does it, Mum? Soon we'll be out of this town for good and then we won't have to see him ever again."

The buzzing chime of her mobile sent shivers shooting up her spine. Her eyes closed and her head lowered, the pain of the evening still fresh in her mind.

Please don't let it be Blake.

She breathed a sigh of relief when Sophie's name flashed across the screen. "Yes, Sophie," she managed to rasp out.

"Tessa. Oh, my God, are you all right?" she rambled down the line.

No, what do you think?

"I'll be fine, Sophie. Eventually," she said with an unhappy sigh.

"I just found out what happened. I can't believe Blake was such a bastard? Serves him right, you should have hit him more than once and aimed for his balls instead of his face."

Tessa smiled at her friend's blunt statement. "I just need some time to myself. I'll call you soon. Okay?"

"Okay, sweetie. Take care. You sure you'll be all right?" she asked one more time.

"Yes. Talk to you soon." Tessa ended the call, turned her phone off and threw it back in her bag. Exhaustion washed over her weary body. Not wanting to be alone, she'd had Isaac drop her at the hospital straight after the dance. Her muscles cramped as she settled in the chair for the night. She tossed and turned, Blake's angry face dominating her dreams.

Tessa's eyes fluttered open under the golden rays of the sunlight streaming through the blinds. She blinked a few times and for a moment, she had no idea where she was or how she'd gotten there. She sat up and pain assaulted her body, robbing her of her next breath. Her screaming body was convincing evidence that she'd slept in the armchair the entire night. She rolled her head and her eyes caught the image of her mother sitting up in bed eating breakfast.

"Good morning, sleepyhead," Lyndall said taking another spoonful of her Corn Pops. "I wondered if you would ever wake up."

"Mum?" Tessa whispered, wide-eyed.

"Yes, Tessa, it's me," she smiled. "You're definitely going to have to do something about that snoring of yours. How are you ever going to get a good night's sleep? It's like listening to a fog horn blasting through a thick morning fog rolling in over the mountains."

Tessa smiled, wincing at the painful twinge in her neck. "You remember me?"

Lyndall huffed. "Well, of course, I remember you, but what are you doing, sleeping in that chair?"

"I...um slept here last night."

Lyndall placed her empty bowl on her lap. "Yes, that much is obvious, but why?"

"I didn't want to go home after the reunion, so I came here to be with you."

Lyndall's brow creased. "Reunion?"

Tessa stretched the creeks and cracks out of her body as she walked around the bed. "Yes, the school restaged our tenth reunion, exactly the same as our original Christmas dance all those years ago, don't you remember?"

She shook her head. "What year is it?"

"It's 2017, Mum," she said worry lines creasing her forehead.

Lyndall paled and her eyes glazed over. "2017? Are you still with Blake?"

Tessa's gut wrenched. The sickly taste of vomit rose in her throat as the fiery image of Blake's angry face filled her mind again. "No, Mum, I'm not with Blake anymore. We haven't been together for six years, since I left to go to London."

She gasped. "Oh, my God."

"It's all right. We've come to an understanding, of sorts."

"I'm so sorry, Tessa."

"Mum, there's nothing to be sorry about. It's just the way it was meant to be."

Lyndall's breath visibly sped up and she shook her head fervently. "No, no it wasn't. It was all my fault."

Concern etched itself in Tessa's heart. "Mum, you need to stay calm. I'm not sure what you're talking about, but—"

Lyndall collected Tessa's hands in hers, pulling her towards the edge of the bed. "I didn't know it would turn out this way. You have to believe me."

"Mum, you're starting to scare me," her voice quivered. "I don't know what you're talking about."

"It was all my fault. You see... I lied," Lyndall said, tears welling in her eyes.

Lied? About what? Tessa felt the blood drain from her face.

"Yes, about Blake. When I first became ill with this awful disease, I tried to ignore the deteriorating effect it was having on me. I was in denial. I didn't want to know about it." She wrapped her arms around her waist in a protective manner. "I didn't tell you because I didn't want you to worry, when your career is so important to you. I love you and I wanted the best for you. But then this disease started to affect my memory and then some of the days blended with others. I have good days and then there are the bad days." She paused. "And I knew I couldn't stop it and it would only get worse."

"Mum," she butted in.

"No," Lyndall snapped. "You must listen while it's fresh in my mind." Tessa nodded. "You need to understand that what I did, I did out of love for you." Tears streamed down her face. "I wanted you to succeed. See your dreams come true and become the actress I always knew you would be, not make the same mistakes I made. I didn't want you to end your career the same way I did…pregnant, with no husband to stand by you."

Her mother's words crushed her heart. "Pregnant? …with me?"

Lyndall nodded. "It's all in the letter I wrote you."

Tears burned the edge of Tessa's eyelids. "Letter, what letter? I didn't get any letter."

Lyndall confessed through stuttered words. "That's because I didn't post it. I wanted to, but then when it came down to it, I just couldn't. It's sitting in the top draw of my sideboard with the letter you asked me to pass on to Blake."

Shock clutched at her throat, ripping the air from her lungs. *Blake didn't get my letter?* Anguish tore through Tessa's body like a burning blaze. "What. Are. You. Saying?"

There was no faking the sorrow in Lyndall's voice and in her eyes. "I'm saying it was me, I'm the one who lied to Blake all those years ago."

"I don't believe what I'm hearing." She closed her eyes and shook her head, numb from head to toe. "How could you lie to me? To Blake? What were you thinking?" she shrieked.

"I was only thinking of you. I wanted to protect you. At the time, I thought it was the only way," she sobbed. "Now I know how wrong I was."

Realisation slammed into Tessa's chest. Her pulse rate kicked up as did her breathing. *Blake was right. Everything he accused me of last night was because he believed* I *was the one who said those horrible lies.* Her knees weakened and she fell down into the chair.

"Tessa?" Lyndall's voice broke through her thoughts.

"No, I don't want to hear anymore." She snarled slamming her hands over her ears. "You destroyed the one good thing in my life. The one thing that I knew without doubt was that I loved Blake and he loved me. No wonder he thinks I'm a manipulating bitch."

"Please, Tessa. I did it out of love for you."

"No, Mum, you did it out of jealously." Adrenaline surged through her veins and her chest burned with anger. "Don't you dare make excuses for your actions. You knew if push came to shove, I would have chosen Blake over my career and you couldn't let that happen, could you?"

"Tessa, please."

"Enough," she yelled, tears clouding her vision. "No wonder Blake was so angry. I've never seen him so angry before in my life."

"He'll forgive you when you tell him the truth."

Tessa wanted to scream the walls down. "I'll be lucky if he lets me in the same room as him, let alone let me speak to him."

"You have a beautiful heart," Lyndall said wiping her moist cheeks with a tissue. "I'm proud and honoured to call you my daughter. I'm just sorry I never said it enough."

Too little, too late, Tessa thought.

"Go to him, tell him it was me who tore you apart. If he doesn't look into your eyes and see the truth, then he doesn't deserve you."

Tessa stood on wobbly knees, her shattered heart heavy with the news of her mum's betrayal.

Lyndall's voice broke through the haze of confusion that bombarded her thoughts. "Tessa?"

"I need to get out of here," she said, grabbing her bag and heading for the door.

"Will you be back?"

She wanted to say no, but this was her mother, the only one she'd ever have. She may not like her right now, but she did love her. "Yes, Mum, I'll be back." She sighed. "Why don't you rest now?"

Lyndall nodded and Tessa closed the door as she left.

She shuddered and leant against the closed door.

Oh, God, I'm no better than she is. Who am I to judge her, when I've been misleading everyone for the past six years?

The apple certainly hadn't fallen far from the tree. She fought the bile churning in her gut ready to show itself at any moment.

Her mother's actions crushed her and she cursed herself for not following her heart in the first place. *No wonder Blake couldn't stand the sight of me.*

Ice struck in her veins, and she knew without doubt exactly what she had to do.

Find out the truth.

Tessa threw her coat on and bolted from the hospital, oblivious to the icy wind that blew. She hailed the first cab she spotted. Her chest was heavy and it felt like it was going to explode.

The letter would have all the answers. *It has to.* Her mind frazzled, she hadn't even noticed the cab pull up outside her house.

"Lady...lady, we're here," his gruff voice called.

"Oh, thank you." Tessa handed him a twenty-dollar bill and fled the cab in haste.

She held her breath and marched straight into her mother's bedroom. Tessa froze in front of the sideboard. The truth, the reason her life fell apart, was an arms-length away. She slowly let out her breath, her head dizzy from holding it in so long.

"Oh, for God's sake, this is ridiculous." She yanked the draw open and grabbed the envelope with her name scrawled across it in Lyndall's handwriting. She ran her trembling fingers over her mother's beautiful penmanship.

No time like the present. Ripping the envelope open, she read as the damning words flew off the page. Her knees buckled and she would have hit the floor if the bed hadn't caught her descent. It was almost too much to comprehend.

"I don't believe this." Each word added to the gut-wrenching pain in her heart. "How could she tell Blake I wouldn't have his children? More to the point, she told him I *couldn't* have children." The sadness overcoming her heart began to turn to anger.

"What the?" Her eyes could hardly believe what she was reading. "I never once said Blake was holding me back or that I never loved him." *I loved him with my whole heart, I still love him.*

Tessa's jaw dropped, and her eyes widened in disbelief. She shot up off the bed. "What the hell?" Rage filled her through and through.

How dare she tell Blake so bluntly that I never loved him and I was using him in every way until I made it in London. I would 'never dump his sorry pathetic arse,' as she so elegantly put it.

Her lungs starved for air. "Jesus Christ," she said running her hand through her hair.

How the hell could you have possibly done this to me, Mum? You obviously loved my career more than my happiness.

The realisation of her mother's actions hit her in the gut like a tonne of bricks. *Blake and I never had a chance.* No amount of words she threw at him would have changed the outcome, the damage was done. Damage she desperately needed to fix, and quickly.

It was her failure. She shook her head, the crush of her stupidity hit her with full force. She should have fought for him, for their love.

Am I too late?

※ ※ ※

Blake tossed around in his bed, the pillows moist from his endless sweating. His head pounded with his need for Tessa. Was he dreaming or was it real? Tessa's naked body entwined in his arms, in his bed, lying skin to skin. Her sensual curves glowing under the fluorescent warmth of the bedside lamp.

"Tessa," he moaned, his head thrashing from side to side.

The constant hammering in his head droned on like church bells that refused to stop ringing. He shot up in his bed and grabbed his throbbing head. "Ahhhhh," he groaned. His breath sped up. "Bloody hell." His head pounded like he had his own personal drummer bashing away inside his mind.

Queasiness erupted deep in his gut. "Yuck," he said. His mouth tasted like a hairy fur ball. Remnants of the night before faded in and out. Scotch, bourbon and more scotch. He groaned and rolled to the side of the bed. Might not have been the best way to wipe last night's scene from his mind. *Damn that woman, I hope she rots in hell.*

How did I get home? He thought rubbing his forehead.

He couldn't remember much past the bourbon. He needed the scotch to wipe away the ugly scene with Tessa, and the bourbon to erase her from his heart. *Forever.* The unpleasant churning in his stomach was a stark reminder of his foolishness.

He buried his head in his hands. *What the hell was I thinking asking her to dance?* That's just it, he wasn't thinking. The moment his eye caught the unruly sight of her raven-black hair swishing around her shoulders he'd been a goner. Her gorgeous plump breasts had been sweetly pushed up to display a generous amount of cleavage for everyone to see, including her precious boyfriend.

His blood boiled when he'd spotted Isaac's hands groping Tessa in front of the entire crowd. Dancing with her was the only thing he could think of to get her away from him...fast.

Blake's hand rubbed his cheek. Anger tightened his jaw. The sting of Tessa's handprint was still as strong in his mind now as it had been the moment it'd made contact with his cheek. He closed his eyes against the sudden burst of rage. *How dare she?*

He jumped at the unexpected chime of the doorbell. He glanced at the clock, *ten o'clock*. "There better be a fucking fire." Still dressed in last night's outfit, he strolled to the door as fast as his pounding head would allow him.

Blake's breath caught in his throat and his heart skipped a beat. His eyes glued to the outline of Tessa's full plum red lips.

"What do you want?"

"We need to talk," she said in a soft voice.

"Talk," he snapped. "*Now*, you want to talk?" Her pupils dilated, and her body froze on the spot. Blake wasn't even sure she was still breathing.

"Y-yes, there are a few things that I need to explain," Tessa stuttered.

"Don't bother. I think we said all we needed to say last night, don't you agree?" Blake blew out his struggling breath.

"No, I don't," she hesitated. "You don't understand."

He barrelled forward, anger bursting from every pore of his body. "Understand...I understand perfectly. You wanted a meal ticket, someone to follow you around like a pathetic little sheep, someone who you could use, chew up and then throw away like a piece of shit. Never mind destroying their heart in the process."

Tears blackened Tessa's eyes. "No, Blake it wasn't me. I know you think it was, but it wasn't. I didn't say all those things. I loved you."

Blake ran a tense hand through his hair. "Give it up, Tessa. If it wasn't you, who was it then?"

"My mother made it all up," Tessa said, barely above a whisper.

"Your mother? Why would she do that?" he balked.

"I didn't know, I swear," she said, her voice growing sombre. "She's the one that lied to you because she knew you were a threat to my career."

He shuddered, her words sliced his heart like a knife. His jaw clenched and he wanted nothing more than to slam the door in her lying smug face.

"So...what you're saying is that you would have given your career up for me?" he said dryly.

She paled and swallowed hard. "Yes. In a heartbeat."

A chill snaked down his spine. "Seriously, will you ever stop with the lies?"

She held her shaky hand out towards him.

"Save it," he spat, eying the paper she held tightly in her hand. "I don't want your apology. I didn't want it then and I don't want it now."

"Blake, I..." She shook her head and lowered her hand, her brow furrowed and tears threatened to undo her before his eyes. "Fine. I was trying to make things right. For what it's worth...I'm sorry."

Sorry, she's sorry. She ripped my heart out and then came back and stomped all over it again and she's sorry.

Blake couldn't breathe. His heart was about to pound right out of his chest. His eyes watched the sexy sway of her hips as she walked away. Again.

Damn it, he wanted to scream at the top of his lungs, but instead he slammed the door with enough anger it shook the windows.

I'm done. Done with Tessa, done with women...Period.

Chapter Five

"OH, HONEY. I'M so sorry," Sophie said, throwing her arms around Tessa as she sobbed into her shoulder.

"He was so angry, Sophie. Furious and I don't blame him," she sobbed throwing her tear-soaked tissue in the kitchen waste bin. "I know what Mum did was wrong, but it was six years ago. I guess too much hurt has happened since then."

"He could have at least listened to you and let you explain," she huffed. "Did you show him the letter?"

Tessa shook her head and wiped her cheek with the back of her hand. "No, I didn't get that far. He wouldn't listen to a word I had to say. Can't blame him really."

"I'm sorry, sweetie. What will you do now?" She asked her brow creased with concern.

"I'm off to Morrisville this evening and I'll be staying there for a while, 'til I can find a permanent place in Burlington," she said in a low, sorrowful voice.

"What? You're not even staying for Christmas?" Sophie gasped.

"I'm sorry, Soph, but I can't stay. Not when I'll run into Blake at every turn. Besides, I need to work and I'm not going to get much around here? Someone's got to pay the bills."

"But what about your mum? I know what she did was wrong, but you can't just leave her in the hospital."

She could feel her anxiety simmering deep in her gut. "No, I won't, she'll be coming with me. Isaac managed to get me an interview at Yarra Pines in Burlington, so that's probably where I'll end up. It's one of the best care facilities for dementia patients. I have a meeting with the manager later this week."

Tessa's hands trembled as she reached into her bag and pulled out the two letters. Her mother's confession and her letter to Blake she wrote six months after she left. Her eyes filled with tears as she held them tight in her hands. "I'll post these on the way home. If he won't listen to my explanation, maybe he will read the truth for himself."

"Are you sure that's wise?"

Tessa's frowned at her friend. "What do you mean?"

"I mean, it's done, over with, finished. Why stir up more feelings and emotions, just to be hurt all over again?"

"He deserves to know the truth, Sophie. I know it won't make any difference, but at least I'll know I did all that I could to make amends."

Oh, Blake, so much time wasted, so much love lost. Nausea welled in the pit of her stomach and she forced herself to maintain composure.

"I suppose you're right." Sophie shrugged.

She was holding it together by the thinnest of threads. The sooner she left town, the sooner she could get her life back on track. Sliding from the kitchen stool she wrapped her arms tightly around Sophie, ignoring the stabbing pain of loss piercing her heart. "I'll shoot off, now. I've got to pack a few things before I head out this evening."

"Okay, sweetie," Sophie said squeezing Tessa in a big sisterly hug. "Do you have somewhere to stay?"

Tessa nodded. "I'm staying with Auntie Nat, in Morrisville. You have her number, don't you?"

Sophie nodded. "Drive carefully. You know what Sunday drivers can be like, heading out of town after the weekend break."

"Yeah, I remember." Tessa moved towards the door. "Take care, Sophie. Love you."

"Love you too. Call me when you get there so I know you made it safely."

Tessa nodded, "I will." The warmth of Sophie's smile bled through her heart.

"What a fucking waste of another day," Blake mumbled to himself dropping his briefcase on the lounge room floor. He didn't make it to work yesterday, thanks to another self-inflicted hangover, and today wasn't much better. Time was running out to get payroll done and the office accounts in order before the banks closed for the Christmas break.

He loosened his tie and removed his suit jacket, flinging both across the back of the lounge in one swift move. He threw himself into his work today, trying in vain to wipe Tessa from his mind. Big mistake. His heart hadn't been in it. Thank God, she had the decency to stay away from him now. He made more fuck-ups today than ever before.

Scanning the mail, the blood in his veins froze. He drew in several breaths, trying to calm his pumping pulse. His hand gripped the letter. *Tessa's letter.* He'd know her handwriting anywhere.

"Fuck." He didn't want to listen to her excuses two days ago, and he damn well didn't want to read them. His fingers itched to rip them into the tinniest of shreds, as she'd done to his heart. Instead, he made quick work of them and tossed them in the bin and headed for a shower.

He braced his hands against the shower wall and let the steaming hot water run down his blazing body. "Damn it, Tessa. Why the hell did you have to come back? Couldn't you have stayed out of my life for good?"

His body remembered the sexy image of her at the reunion. Just thinking about her in that red dress or more to the point, out of it. God, he wanted her. He wanted her so badly, even more than his next breath. His rock-hard cock, a reminder of what she could do to him, which no other woman had managed to achieve. And then there was Isaac.

Rage. Red hot rage seared through his every nerve ending. He saw red the moment Isaac had place his arm around Tessa. His face whitened at the realisation. He was jealous, jealous of Isaac.

Why the hell would I be jealous? Why is she the only woman that gets me so excited and pissed off in the same breath?

He'd been so deep in thought that he hadn't even realised his body was shivering under a cold stream of water. Barely drying himself, he wrapped the towel around the lower half and stormed out to the kitchen and retrieved Tessa's letter from the rubbish bin.

"This stops, now," he said, eyeing the letter. "I'm done with your lies and manipulations. I'll read your damn letters and then this will be over for good."

Blake ripped it open and a folded letter and an unopened envelope drifted to the floor. He snatched them up. His eyes stung as he read the date on the envelope.

2011? His pulse raced. *It's dated the same year that she left Whittaker Springs.*

"Then, what's this other one?"

He unfolded it. Each word tore through his heart like a machete slicing through sugar cane. Blake frowned and his breathing sped up. *It was true.* Lyndall's confession. She's the one that manipulated both of them, played them against each other. It was hard to control the rage that mounted with each word that screamed at him from the page.

Blake's face grew stormier. "What the... Why the fuck would she do that? She had to know how much I loved her daughter and that I would have followed her to the ends of the earth." He froze to the spot, paralysed with a multitude of emotions. Anger, grief, fear and regret.

Blake's knees began to tremble and he sat down at the kitchen bench before he fell down. All this time he'd blamed Tessa. He misdirected his anger. He closed his eyes to the pain and he hung his head. The vicious words he threw at her at the reunion bombarded his mind.

Manipulative, lying, deceitful tactics...pretending to be in love with me, pretending to want to have my children, was really beneath even a sexy seductress like you.

Nausea hit him and he thought he would be sick. Oh, God, then again Sunday morning, she tried to make things right and he'd thrown it back in her face again. She tried to tell him it was her mother, but he'd shot her down and wouldn't have a bar of it.

He dropped his head in his hands and squeezed his eyes shut. He wanted to scream, roar from the highest mountain. Six long miserable years wasted. He gagged at the foul bile rising in his mouth. He deserved no less.

Blake's eyes opened and landed on Tessa's letter. His heart plummeted. He forced himself to sit and read her words. He was utterly numb with shock.

"...I've made the biggest mistake of my life, Blake. I love you and only you, much more than my career and I know that now. I should have trusted in us, believed in us. Coming to London was a huge mistake, but more than that, is knowing that I destroyed our love and that's something I'll regret for the rest on my life.

I want to come home. If you'll still have me and if you can forgive me for not following my heart. I want a life with you, have your children and grow old with you and no one else. The number where I'm staying is below, if you can see it in your heart to forgive me. I hope I hear from you.

All my love forever.

Tessa ☺

Each word crushed Blake's chest like he'd been hit with a truck load of bricks. The realisation hit thick and fast. *I never knew. She'd waited for me to ring and I never did.* The tears that he'd tried so hard to suppress ran freely down his cheeks. He struggled to comprehend the years he'd spent angry and hurt by her departure when he could have had her here, in his arms, in his life forever.

She tried to make it right Sunday morning, but his pig-headedness wouldn't let her explain. *Damn it, when you fuck up, you fuck up big, don't you?* His gut clenched, remembering the devastation on her face when he'd turned her away. God, he was such a prick.

Steely determination flooded his veins. He loved her, always had and always will. Was it too late? Blake bolted into his bedroom, his heart pounding inside his ribcage. Dressed within seconds, he grabbed his keys and wasted no time heading out to make amends. He just hoped she would listen to his apology and not slam the door in his face as he had done to her, no matter how much he deserved it.

Blake pulled up outside Tessa's house, the tyres screeching to a holt. He bolted to the door ringing the doorbell several times. His heart felt like it was going to jump right out of his chest.

No answer.

He bashed on the door with his fist. "Tessa...Tessa are you there? It's Blake." Fire ignited in his chest and he waited impatiently for an answer. "Tessa...Tessa," he yelled.

"Blake, what on earth are you doing?" Suzanne, Lyndall's neighbour called from her front porch. "You're going to get yourself in trouble with the police, if you're not careful."

Suzanne, thank God. Blake rushed over taking her front steps two at a time. "Suzanne, I'm looking for Tessa. It's really important that I find her. Do you know where she is?"

She frowned. "She's gone."

His chest seized. "Gone?"

"Yes, afraid so," she said.

"What do you mean gone?" —he was too late— "Where did she go?" A sinking feeling of doom rooted itself in his gut.

"I'm not sure, love." She grimaced. "She packed her suitcase in her car Sunday evening and said goodbye."

He fought the devastating crush inside his chest. *She was gone.* He'd lost her. "Thanks, Suzanne."

"I'm sorry I can't be more help."

Blake bolted back to his car. *You might not be, but I know someone who can.*

※ ※ ※

Sophie stood at her front door and glared at Blake through slitted eyes. "No. I am not telling you where she is."

"Oh, come on, Sophie," Blake pleaded. "I need to see her."

Sophie shook her head. "No, no way. Don't you think you've hurt her enough, Blake? She tried to make things right and you shut her down, crushed her like an ant. This would have been the first Christmas that we would have celebrated together in forever and you screwed it up. So, as far as I'm concerned, you can fuck off."

His chest ached and his heart hurt, but he wasn't giving up. Blake shoved his foot between the doorframe and the door. Sophie jumped back as he palmed the door open. "I am not leaving here until you tell me where she is. I know you know."

Sophie shot daggers at him and folded her arms across her chest. "Why the hell should I?"

He sighed. Renewed determination coursed through his veins. "Because I was wrong. I should have let her explain and because of my selfish, pig-headedness I may have lost the only women I have ever loved and I *do* love her, Sophie with all my heart."

Sophie's mouth dropped open and her eyes stared at Blake's solemn face.

"Please, I just want to apologise if she'll let me, and then if she throws me out and never wants to see my ugly face again, I promise I'll leave her alone to get on with her life. But at least she'll know that she can come back and be with you for Christmas without any interference from me."

Sophie rolled her eyes to the roof and huffed. "I think we both know that you're far from ugly."

A glimmer of hope seeped into Blake's heart. "Please, Sophie," he said, his voice hushed and calm. "I've wasted too much time away from her. I'll fight for her love—Isaac and any other man who thinks he can love her more than I can."

Sophie giggled. "Wait, you think Tessa and Isaac are a couple?"

He frowned and nodded slowly.

"Man, you do have some apologising to do you dumbass." She shook her head in disgust. "They're just friends. Isaac is Lyndall's nurse."

"Nurse?" His relief plastered all over his face.

She nodded. "Yes, her nurse and they're just friends."

Her eyes bore into his and the silence between them unsettled his stomach until his insides were tied in knots. "Come on, Sophie."

"All right," she said throwing her arms up in the air in resignation. "But I swear to God, if you so much as hurt her again, I'll be after you like there's no tomorrow and I'll make you suffer. I'll cut off your balls and feed them to Harry's pigs for supper. You got me?"

Blake swallowed the golf-ball sized lump in his throat. With his manhood in jeopardy, he wasn't about to make any more wrong moves. "I understand completely, but you don't have to worry. I'm in this forever, if Tessa will have me."

The corner of Sophie's mouth turned up into a smile. "Wait here, I'll be right back."

It was less than a few minutes before she returned and handed him a piece of paper. "She's staying at her Aunt Nat's, in Morrisville until she can find somewhere to live in Burlington."

Burlington? Not if I can help it. "Thanks, Sophie," he said, slotting the paper into his jacket.

"Blake…" Sophie paused and waited for their eyes to lock. "Just don't hurt her again."

"I promise you, that's the last thing I'm going to do. I love her and I'm going to spend the rest of my life proving it."

Sophie smiled and closed the door as he left.

Tessa threw her bag on the bed and flopped back, exhausted. Every muscle in her body ached, not to mention her pounding head. Who knew job hunting could be so tiring?

Her Aunt Nat was away this week on a book tour in New York. Tessa had the house all to herself. Thank goodness. Being the professional health freak that Nat was, she would never have approved of how inebriated Tessa had been last night. She almost hadn't made it to the toilet before she'd thrown up the copious amount of wine she'd consumed.

The meeting at Yarra Pines couldn't have gone smoother and Isaac was right, it was an amazing facility. So why did she feel so disheartened? She wanted to curl up in a little ball and slip into oblivion, leaving all her problems and broken heart behind.

She sat up and winced as she flicked her shoes off. "Ouch," she moaned rubbing her feet one at a time. "Whoever invented high-heel shoes should be held up in front of a firing squad and shot." She'd managed to email her resume into a dozen or so businesses today, which was better than nothing. Tomorrow, she'd try again.

By the time the oven bell went off, she'd had a shower and slipped into her comfy Peter Alexander pyjamas. With a plate of pizza and a glass of chilled wine in hand, she was set for another pathetic night in. "This is living the high life now." She laughed to herself.

Sufficiently stuffed from over-eating, she dozed off just as the *NCIS* theme music boomed from the television. She jumped, startled by the chime of the doorbell. Disorientated, she bolted upright, her pulse drumming inside her chest. The doorbell rang again. *What the...? Who the hell would be calling this late at night?* There it was again. "Well, whoever it is, is obviously not going away."

She flicked the peephole open and froze. She swallowed hard, as if she could barely draw in enough air to breathe. *Blake. No, no, no it can't be. What is he doing here?* She slammed shut the peephole and stepped back away.

She stared at the closed door. Anxiety, worry and concern etched itself in every muscle of her body. Battling to stay in control, she sucked in deep breaths.

"Tessa." Blake's voice boomed through the door.

Tessa couldn't breathe. It was simply too much. She'd resigned herself to never seeing him again and now he was standing less than two meters away.

"Tessa, if you're in there and can hear me, please open the door I just want to talk." The agony and desperation in his voice spoke to her heart.

"Tessa, I'm not leaving until you hear me out. If I have to talk through this wooden door then that's what I'll do, but I would much prefer to look into your beautiful eyes."

Tessa's breath caught in her throat. Tears welled in her eyes. She squeezed them shut, unsure if she was in a dream or a nightmare.

"Tessa, please, I promise that all I want to do is talk. I owe you an apology."

An apology? She shook her head in silent confusion and eased the door open a few inches. A knot formed in her throat stripping her of the ability to communicate. Her heart sped up at the sight of him.

"Blake, I—"

He took a steely step forward. "No, Tessa, let me. I have a lot to say."

She paused.

"May I come in? I promise I just want to talk."

She finally nodded and opened the door. She wouldn't be able to speak past the knot in her throat anyway.

"Tessa," he sighed. The pain in his eyes was as deep as the wound to her heart. "God, you're so beautiful," he whispered, his eyes bore into her soul. "I'm not sure where to start."

She gasped and her hand went to her throat as he held up her letters. Reluctantly, she lifted her gaze to his. "You read them?" she whispered.

"Yes, I read them." He took another step towards her. "There are no words to describe how sorry I am for the things I said to you. I don't know why your mother did what she did, but I do know that she loves you and you can't fault a mother's love. They'll do anything to protect their children."

Tears streaked down her cheeks as his beautiful words sunk in.

"I blamed you for so long," he said, brushing her hair from her face. "Blamed you for destroying my heart.

I was bitter and angry and I'm so sorry. More than words can say."

"Oh, Blake," she cried. "I'm sorry too. That's why I wrote you. I knew I'd made a terrible mistake." She buried her tearful face in her hands and sobbed.

"Hey, shh...shh," he said, easing his arms around her trembling body. "I know, and if I had gotten your letter, I would have been on the first plane to London to find you and wrap you in my arms and my heart."

Tessa sighed, lulled by his light caresses. She gave herself over to his soft touch. She mumbled into his chest between hiccups. "I wish we could go back and erase the past six years and start again."

"We can't erase it, but we can learn from it. I've made so many wrong choices over the years, but the one thing I know for sure is that I love you, Tessa Quinn. I always have and I always will."

Tessa couldn't breathe. She froze in his embrace, barely able to draw air into her lungs.

He loves me... Still.

Awareness snaked up her spine, despite her attempts to keep it at bay. He nudged her chin up and she knew he felt it too. Her eyes widened, and she centred on Blake's eyes until she felt herself falling into the deep pools of his irises.

Slowly, as if they were moving in slow motion his lips were centimetres from hers. His breath brushed across her sensitive lips. "Tessa, it's been too long since I've had you in my arms. I can't wait any longer."

"Wait for what?" she said, barely above a whisper.

His mouth descended on hers. Soft, delicate and hot, oh so hot. Tessa's heart raced under the tender touch of his lips. Tears stung her eyes, happy tears.

Blake's tongue delved inside her mouth and she opened for him. His taste so potent her head swam with dizziness. She pressed in and his arms tightened around her firmly telling her that she was his, now and forever. She moaned into his mouth, a moan of desire. His feather light kisses spread over her cheek, jawbone and down her neck and then over her earlobes.

His lips sent an electric jolt of energy through her entire body. The feathery strokes of his tongue were driving her insane. His lips were better than she remembered.

"I don't care about the past. It doesn't matter anymore," he whispered against her skin. "What matters is the future. Our future together, and that we have a clean slate from this day forward. I don't care if you want to live in Burlington, Whittaker Spring or on the other side of the world. As long as I'm with you, that's all that matters."

Blake pressed his lips over each of her moist eyelids and kissed away her tears. "We'll sort the rest out as it comes, but one thing I'm not prepared to comprise on is you. I love you, Tessa."

"Oh, Blake, I love you too." She smiled through her happy tears. "I've never stopped loving you. I want you now and forever."

"Sounds good to me." He smiled and fused his lips to her once more.

Oh, yes, the future was definitely looking brighter.

Thank you for reading **Christmas Fever**

If you enjoyed this story, I would really appreciate it if you would consider leaving a review of this book, no matter how short, at the retailer site where you bought your copy or on sites like Amazon or Goodreads.

YOU are the key to this book's success. I read every review and they really do make a huge difference.

Keep up to date on P.L. Harris' book releases, signings and events on Facebook:
https://www.facebook.com/plharrisauthor
Follow P.L. Harris Readers Group:
https://www.facebook.com/groups/217817788798223
Website: http://www.plharris.com.au

About the Author

P.L. Harris writes contemporary romance, romantic suspense and young/new adult with a twist of mystery and intrigue. P.L. writes cozy mysteries for those that like to play amateur detective from the comfort of their own homes.

Her books are rich in storyline and location with characters that stay with you long after you turn the last page.

P.L. Harris is an award winning author. *Hidden Secrets* was a finalist in the Oklahoma Romance Writers of America's 2017 IDA International Digital Awards, young adult category. *Callie's Dilemma* was also a finalist in the Virginia Romance Writers of America's 2017 Fools of Love Contest, short contemporary romance short category.

She lives in the northern suburbs of Perth, Western Australia, with her Bishon Frise, Bella. When *P.L's* not writing or reading, she enjoys spending time with her family and experiencing what Perth has to offer. You can visit *P.L. Harris* at her website: www.plharris.com.au

Read on for an excerpt of Book 1 of
The Cupcake Series – Cupcakes and Cyanide

Book 1 – Cupcakes and Cyanide

Welcome to Ashton Point. One sweet taste could be her last.

Charlotte McCorrson has spent her entire life building her business, CC's Simply Cupcakes. The town of Ashton Point is her home and she's garnered a reputation of stellar service and delightful pastries, one nibble at a time. But everything isn't as sweet in the sleepy, coastal town as Charlotte would like to think. She is in for a rude awakening and no amount of sugar will make this medicine go down any smoother.

After catering a large town-wide event, Ashton Point's morning newspaper fills Charlotte McCorrson with an icy sense of dread. The headlines scream *Cupcake Killer!* and put the blame squarely on CC's Simply Cupcakes. When bodies begin to pile up behind her confectionary goodies, Charlotte must prove that while her cupcakes are delicious, they aren't literally to die for—before she ends up in jail for a crime she didn't commit.

Read on for an excerpt of book 1

Cupcakes and Cyanide

Chapter One

"CALLING ALL THE single ladies."

Charlotte McCorrson stood nestled at the back of the reception centre, semi-hidden behind a burgundy-and-white, balloon topiary tree.

Great. Bouquet throwing time, just what I need. For every man in the room to know I'm still single. When Beth invited her to the wedding she was over the moon, after all they'd been good friends since Clair and her family moved to Ashton Point three years ago. What she hadn't planned on was still being single by the time the wedding rolled around.

They may as well take out a front-page ad in the Ashton Point Chronicle. She could see it now. "Ashton Point master cupcake baker extraordinaire struggles to snag herself a husband. Could she be lacking that special ingredient all men are looking for? What is wrong with the redheaded beauty?" She'd been over the moon when Beth and Lincoln asked CC's Simply Cupcakes to design a wedding cake, based around Charlotte's award-winning cupcake designs.

"Charlotte? What are you doing back here?" A petite voice spoke from behind.

She spun, her breath catching as her gaze landed on a vision in white. Decked out in a satin Karen Willis Holmes, floor-length, empire dress with embroidered tulle overlay, Beth looked like an angel. There had barely been a dry eye in the church as she walked down the aisle to her handsome prince. The fairy-tale wedding every bride dreams of.

Charlotte stiffened as Beth threw her arms around her neck and squeezed. "I never got a chance to properly thank you for the wonderful cupcake display you made. It was truly the cake of my dreams. I'm so glad you were able to share my special day with me. It wouldn't have been the same without you and Clair here," she said with a beaming smile.

"You're welcome, I wouldn't have missed it for the world. I'm so happy you liked it," she said in a muffled voice. Her mouth was half covered by blonde ruffles of hair, leaving the metallic taste of hairspray on her tongue.

Beth pulled back and their gazes held strong. "Liked it? Are you serious? I loved it." A bolt of electric energy ran up Charlotte's spine. She cherished the buzz she got from seeing the joy her cupcakes brought others. "And if anyone thinks they're taking the leftovers home tonight, they have another thing coming. That's all I'll be eating 'til we leave for our honeymoon next week."

Both ladies burst into laughter. Beth's happiness was starting to rub off on Charlotte.

"Didn't you hear the MC? You need to get to the dance floor. I'm about to throw the bouquet."

Charlotte cringed at the thought. "No, no, it's fine. I'm really okay sitting back and letting someone else take the limelight." She had planned on falling madly in love with the man of her dreams by the wedding. *I guess life doesn't always go to plan.*

A sliver of disappointment marred Beth's expression. "I can't believe what I'm hearing. Your grandma would be turning in her grave if she knew you were skipping the bouquet toss. You know how she loved tradition."

Warmth filled Charlotte's heart. Her grandmother treasured her independence. She was the reason they'd moved to Ashton Point in the first place.

She shook her head. "I'm happy watching from the sidelines, besides, a mosh pit of single woman jumping around like clucking chickens, all vying for their piece of the illusive dream isn't really my idea of fun."

"Now, that's something I'd like to see." A gruff voice echoed in her ear.

"Excuse me?" Charlotte said, spinning to see Lincoln's best man grinning like the Cheshire cat.

"A mosh pit of single woman jumping around like clucking chickens," he said with a cheeky grin. "Definitely something I'd pay money to see."

Beth sighed, rolled her eyes and play-punched him in the shoulder. "Give it a rest, Liam."

Liam… Mmmm. Why is it that all men named Liam are gorgeous? Liam Hemsworth, Liam Neeson. Tanned, tall and handsome, he flashed a half smile at Charlotte and she felt a spike of interest spark in her belly.

Her gaze caught her sister, Clair, waving frantically behind Liam. *Saved by the bell.* "I'm sorry, Beth but it looks like Clair needs me."

"Charlotte, there you are. I've been looking for you everywhere," Clair said as she joined them, flicking her deep-red ponytail over her shoulder.

"Why, is something wrong?" Alarm hit Charlotte square in the chest. "Please don't tell me we've run out of cupcakes? There should be plenty to go around. I made loads of extras."

Beth folded her arms across her chest and frowned. "Yes, don't tell me we ran out, otherwise the Bridezilla I've kept hidden inside might have to make a guest appearance."

"Bridezilla?" Liam said with a raised eyebrow. "I find that very hard to believe."

"When it comes to Charlotte's cupcakes, you better believe it," she snapped, holding his stern gaze in hers.

"Everyone clam down, there are plenty of cupcakes." Clair smiled and looped her arm through her sisters. "I was looking for Charlotte for the bouquet toss. Nothing better than a little competition between sisters."

A grin spread across Beth's face and she clapped her hands together. "Wonderful. I best go and get ready. Good luck." Beth said as she hurried off.

"This should be a sight to see. I'll let you two ladies get ready. I'd hate to be the one to keep you from your spot in the chicken brood," Liam said with a smile as he strode back to the bridal table at the top of the dance floor.

Clair raised an eyebrow. "Chicken brood?"

"Never mind," Charlotte said, shaking her head.

"Wasn't that the best man?" Clair asked, forcefully guiding Charlotte toward the crowded dance floor.

Charlotte nodded. *Certainly was THE best man.* She let her eyes wonder over his retreating figure. Her gaze seemed to have a mind of its own. It made its way down his broad shoulders, to his trim waist and tight derriere. She felt her cheeks grow hot as she imagined what he would look like out of his suit.

"What was his name again?" Clair's words were met with silence. "Earth to Charlotte," she said, flicking Charlotte's forehead as if she were flicking a fly from the back of her hand. "What is his name?" she snapped.

"Oww." Charlotte's rubbed her forehead. "All right. I heard you the first time. Liam. His name is Liam."

Charlotte's stomach tightened as Clair elbowed their way to the centre of the dance floor dragging her along for the ride.

"Okay, ladies. Are we ready for the bouquet toss?" The deep, throaty voice of the MC's blared out across the room.

Charlotte's body tensed as ear-splitting screams of single women pierced the air. *Oh my, could this be any more embarrassing?*

To top it off, Beyoncé's *Single Ladies* boomed out as Beth took centre stage.

Her breath caught in her throat as her gaze snared Liam's sly grin from the front of the room. *What's with the grin?* Cheers erupted around her and her eyes widened as Beth's bouquet flew straight into her arms.

Charlotte stood in the kitchen, her lungs void of air as the newspaper headline screamed at her like unwanted nightmare. She held the morning newspaper in her icy fingers. *Cupcake Killer!*

Beth's wedding had been the event of the year, a perfect place to show off her culinary skills. The whole town had turned up to see her finally tie the knot with Lincoln Wade, Ashton Point's most eligible bachelor. Everyone who's anyone had been there, which meant more advertising for their business, CC's Simply Cupcakes.

"I don't believe this." Her hands shook as she read the front-page article. Definitely not the front page she had imagined last night at the wedding. "Why would they think *my* cupcakes killed someone?"

Her eyes were glued to the quote at the bottom of the page next to her picture. *Doctor says two beloved local councilmen are in critical condition and show signs of cyanide poisoning.*

"Cyanide poisoning?" she asked, collapsing on the kitchen stool as her knees gave way. "I do *not* cook with cyanide."

She continued to read. *Guests say that they began feeling ill after the cake was cut and cupcakes distributed.*

"Definitely not from my cupcakes." Anger simmered in her veins. It was going to hit the fan, so to speak, when her sister, Clair, heard of this debacle. Thankfully Cassidy was over visiting Mum and Dad in New York for the next two weeks. "At least she won't be tarnished by this nightmare."

This town was their home. They'd moved to Ashton Point on the central coast of New South Wales, just over three years ago to help her grandma. "As if anyone would think I would intentionally poison someone. This is totally unfair." she said, slamming the paper down on the breakfast bar. Her stomach bottoming out as her gaze spotted the bouquet on the kitchen bench.

Clair's weary voice made Charlotte's breath catch in her throat. "What's unfair?" she asked, as she entered the kitchen.

Charlotte's chest tightened like it was being forcibly crushed in a vice. *Damn it, there's no hiding this now.* She scooped up the newspaper before Clair spotted the disaster that was about to tear their dreams apart.

"What's unfair?" Clair repeated heading toward the Nespresso machine wiping the crusty sleep remnants from the inner rim of her eyes.

Charlotte's pulse sped up. Clearing her throat, she stood and held the newspaper close to her chest, ready to face the music head on. "I've something to show you, but maybe you should get a coffee and sit down first." Clair was like a five-foot-five, grumpy bed monster with a tooth ache before her morning coffee.

"For goodness sake, Charlotte, spit it out," she said running her hand through her knotted hair. "I didn't exactly get much sleep last night, by the time we packed up after the wedding."

Charlotte cringed at the mention of the wedding. "You're going to hear about it one way or another." She sighed. "May as well be before you leave the house."

Suspicion worked its way across Clair's face. Leaning against the counter, she folded her arms across her chest. "Okay, enough with the cryptic clues and just tell me what you're talking about."

Charlotte's heart plummeted to the base of her gut. She flipped the paper around and held her breath. Waiting for the incoming explosion.

"Cupcake killer!" Clair's amused, bubbly giggle shot through Charlotte like a dagger. "That's ridiculous. We've known Daniel for three years and everyone in town knows he's big on sensationalising stories without getting his facts straight first. You're not taking that serious, are you?"

"Of course I'm taking it serious."

"It's just Daniel trying to big note his career. You and I know there's no truth to it and I'm sure when the truth is revealed, Daniel will be eating his own words." Clair busied herself working her mass of deep-red, bushy hair into a messy bun on the top of her head. "I'm sure it will blow over once they've worked out how they were really poisoned."

Shock bolted through Charlotte's body. "I can't believe you're being so blasé about this. We've worked out butts off to make CC's Simply Cupcakes the best it can possibly be and…" She paused, fury running through her veins. She shook the newspaper in front of Clair's unimpressed expression. "…bad publicity is the last thing we need." Charlotte's stomach grumbled as the fresh scent of roasted hazelnut assaulted her nostrils.

Clair made two fresh cups and handed one off to Charlotte. "Okay, I suppose this isn't ideal, but I'd hardly think one article in the local rag is going to destroy our business. Besides, the whole town knows Daniel will bend the truth to sell one more newspaper."

Clair skimmed over the article. A myriad of emotions flashing across Clair's face made it impossible for Charlotte to determine her thoughts. "They say that no accusations will be acted upon until they have concrete evidence and they'll be following up all leads. Maybe we should keep our eyes and ears open, just in case."

Anxiety crept into Charlotte's mind and compounded her sudden headache into a dull roar. "I agree, but…"

Clair continued, oblivious to Charlotte's annoyance. "And we have Mrs Stevenson's eightieth birthday high tea tomorrow afternoon, down by the river. I'm sure after that goes off without a hitch, Daniel will not only be eating his words, but also your delicious cupcakes."

"Maybe you're right, but I don't think we should wait for the fall out from this article. I know Beth was taking the leftovers home and I don't want her to worry, so I'm going to head over to reassure them that my cupcakes were not the source of the poisoning."

Clair fake coughed. "The morning after their wedding?"

Frustration bubbled up, sending Charlotte's pulse racing. Again. "They're not leaving for their honeymoon 'til Wednesday, and if I remember rightly, Lincoln has to work today to tie up loose ends before they leave."

She glanced one last time at the newspaper and huffed. *This is the most ludicrous thing ever put in print. I'll make you eat your words, if it's the last thing I do.*

Clair sighed. "Okay, but don't take too long. I'll be heading over to the shop soon to update the books and make sure we have enough supplies for Mrs Stevenson's order. I'll see you when you get there."

"Okay." Inside, she was furious at Clair's nonchalant attitude. "Mark my words, I'll get to the bottom of this."

Annoyed at the incessant interruption to his morning breakfast, Liam Bradly strutted toward the door. A continuous thunderous roar hammered his head, thanks to his addiction to good wine. He'd stupidly over-indulged at the wedding and his queasy stomach was a stark reminder of why he usually drank red instead of white wine.

He ran his hand through his hair and glanced at the wall clock. "Are you serious? It's not even nine o'clock yet. Who the hell visits this early on a Saturday morning, especially after a late wedding reception the night before?" He'd tear strips off whatever idiot was on the other side of the door.

Liam threw the oak door wide open. "Do you have any idea what time…" He froze mid-sentence, his eyes glued to the petite woman standing before him. He'd remember her anywhere. As if he'd forget a woman of her beauty. Her wavy red locks hung just below her shoulders, framing her face. This was much better than the semi-business look she'd wore yesterday at the wedding, hair pulled back in a tight bun. Now, she was the picture of a woman that would tantalise any man, including him.

She's beautiful.

A soft smile curved her lips, but her eyes told a different sorry. The drumming in his head shot his mind back to the present. He smiled. "Well, well, if it isn't the Cupcake Killer in person."

She gasped. "You read it too?"

He nodded. "I'm sure everyone in a town's read it. Hard not to see it. It was plastered all over the front page."

Her eyes widened and her glossy, sapphire-blue pupils deepened. Thrusting her hands on her hips she said, "That article is utter nonsense. They had no right to print that without any evidence. My cupcakes were not the reason those people got sick."

"Really?" he asked folding his arms across his chest and giving her an uninterrupted view of his taut biceps and clenched abs.

Her jaw dropped to speak, but nothing came out. The only indication that she was still breathing was the warm, crimson blush that had worked its way from her neck to her cheeks.

"I...um... I wanted to...um..." She bit her bottom lip and paused mid-sentence as if her voice had suddenly vanished.

What the hell is with her eyes? Their constant flittering movement, combined with his throbbing head, were making him nauseous. It was as if she didn't know where to look.

He was standing there with the door wide open for the whole neighbourhood to see in only his pyjama bottoms. A rush of triumph surged through his system. *Nice to know my body can still affect a woman that way.*

He gestured toward his lack of attire. "My apologies, I wasn't expecting visitors," he said as he waved her inside. "Come in while I get something more appropriate on."

She shook her head. "I'm fine. I just wanted to speak to Beth, if she was around."

Liam turned and headed back inside. "Happy to chat after I get dressed. Close the door after you come in will you?"

He hurriedly dressed and walked into the kitchen, half expecting her not to be there. But there she was, standing in front of the sliding glass door framed by the morning glow of the sun. She looked naturally beautiful in a quiet, understated way.

He shoved his hands in his trouser pockets. "Don't tell me… you've decided to cook me breakfast. I'm not sure my stomach can handle one of your delicious cyanide cupcakes this morning."

She spun and stared straight through him. It unnerved him. Colour leached from her face, leaving her white as a sheet. Stepping back, she stumbled.

Liam let out a string of curses as he lunged for her before she face-planted on the kitchen tiles.

"I'm sorry. That was meant to be a joke. Obviously in poor taste," he said, still holding her elbow and refusing to let go until he was sure she had both feet planted firmly on the ground. Liam rubbed the elbow he'd grabbed, trying to alleviate any discomfort he may have caused by his firm grip.

"Yes, poor taste, indeed," she said huskily, easing her arm from his hold.

"It seems we were both rather busy at the wedding yesterday, and after your triumph in the bouquet toss, you disappeared. We never got the chance to formally meet." He held his hand out, eager for the introduction. "I'm Liam Bradly."

She looked at him in bewilderment, as if he were speaking gibberish, then stepped back and thrust her hand out in his direction, clearly determined to keep him at arms-length. "Charlotte McCorrson."

He smiled and shook her hand. "Nice to meet you, Charlotte." His hand pulsed under her warm touch. A soft smile curved her lips, her eyes glittering under the morning sun.

She withdrew her hand from his grip. "I didn't know you were staying here. I actually came over to see Beth. I wanted to reassure her my cakes were not the source of the poisoning and that article is utter garbage."

"Well, as you can see she's not here, or Lincoln for that matter. They left for their honeymoon in the early hours of this morning, but I'm sure they wouldn't believe it anyway."

"Oh," she said anxiously. "I thought they weren't leaving 'til Wednesday?"

"My surprise wedding gift," Liam said. It was the least he could do for his best friend.

"Are you house sitting for them?" Her eyebrows went up in question.

House sitting? The thought would have most certainly filled him with dread. That was before he met Charlotte. Now the idea had merit. *I have holidays due, and Lincoln did say to make myself at home before they left.* A week relaxing in this quiet town, getting to know the locals, one in particular, was definitely preferable to heading back to Perth to his mundane job of counting numbers on people's tax returns.

"Yes, I'll be house sitting while they're on their honeymoon. Maybe you can show me around town while I'm here," he said flashing her his cheekiest smile.

She gave him a peculiar look, apprehension entering her gaze. She shook her head. "I'm sorry, I can't. I have to get to the bottom of this poisoning before my entire business is ruined."

"Why would someone want to ruin your business?" he pried.

Annoyance washed over her expression. "As if I would know. It's not like we have enemies in town. I'm sure it's all a big misunderstanding."

He was up for an adventure. "Maybe we could make a deal. You show me around town and I'll help you solve the mystery of the cyanide bandit, what do you say?"

Charlotte froze, panic firing her eyes. She hastily moved past him and headed for the door. "I'm sorry, I can't. Enjoy your stay in Ashton Point."

Her rejection felt like a punch to the stomach. By the time he got his thoughts together she was gone. "What the hell just happened?"

Book 2 – Cupcakes and Curses
Murder and cupcakes, a deadly mix.

Clair McCorrson has spent the last three years building her business, CC's Simply Cupcakes with her sister gaining a reputation for mouth-watering excellence in their seaside town of Ashton Point. While Charlotte is the master baker, Clair keeps the business side looking sweet, and if everything goes as planned, she'll be more than the girl behind the scenes.

Expanding their business to the nearby town of Watson's Creek is Clair's idea, and acquiring the Sweets Mansion is her dream come true, her chance to step out from her sister's shadow and make it on her own. Clair's excitement quickly turns sour when she stumbles across the murdered body of local settlement agent.

Newspaper headlines screaming *Cupcake Killer Strikes Again!* Clair's life seems to be going from bad to worse when rumours of the cursed Mansion begin to surface igniting chaos among the locals. Bodies literally begin to mount up around CC's Simply Cupcakes and all the evidence points to Clair. Wrongly accused of murder, it's a race against time to find the real culprit before she spends the rest of her life behind bars.

Book 3 – Cupcakes and Corpses

When it comes to design, death is in the details.

Cassidy McCorrson has worked hard to develop her reputation as a leading interior designer in her seaside town of Ashton Point. Since arriving home from visiting her parents in New York, her skills have been in high demand. Between juggling the design for her sister's new cupcake shop and her private client, Cassidy barely has time to prepare for the upcoming Christmas celebrations.

Cassidy is excited at the prospect of delivering designs she can be proud of, but her world is turned upside down when the body of a local reporter is found murdered on location at her latest work site. What should have been a straightforward job turns out to be the worst decision of her life.

In order to clear her name and restore her reputation, Cassidy must find the real killer before she ends up redesigning the interior of a jail cell. Can she unearth the killer before time runs out?

CPSIA information can be obtained
at www.ICGtesting.com
Printed in the USA
FSHW02n0028210918
52202FS